SIXGUN SHOWDOWN

After years as a lawman elsewhere, Dan Herrick had returned to his old Arizona stamping ground. But the once bustling town Dan had left was no longer. Nesters were being driven from their homesteads, forced out by ruthless ranchers. Danger couldn't be avoided, and swung by his loyalty to a girl named Dorcas, Dan came down on the side of the farmers. Before putting away his own gun once and for all, he forced a bloody and decisive showdown.

ART FLYNN

SIXGUN SHOWDOWN

Complete and Unabridged

LINFORD
Leicester

First published in Great Britain in 1994 by
Robert Hale Limited
London

First Linford Edition
published 1997
by arrangement with
Robert Hale Limited
London

British Library CIP Data

Flynn Art
Sixgun showdown.—Large print ed.—
Linford western library
1. English fiction—20th century
2. Large type books
I. Title
823.9'14 [F]

ISBN 0–7089–5006–X

Published by
F. A. Thorpe (Publishing) Ltd.
Anstey, Leicestershire
Set by Words & Graphics Ltd.
Anstey, Leicestershire
Printed and bound in Great Britain by
T. J. Press (Padstow) Ltd., Padstow, Cornwall

1

THE corpse sprawled face down on the trail and the buzzards were working on it. As Dan Herrick angled his bronc down the ridge, they flapped away on obscenely creaking wings and settled in the sun-split rocks nearby to watch and wait.

The sun of early summer in Arizona slammed down on the land and bounced a shimmering heat-gaze off the ochre slope down which Herrick rode. He was tall, lean as a lost dog and his gear was punished by travel. His black sombrero put a bar of shade across the steel-grey eyes which had been fixed on the dead man and the birds of prey since he spotted them from the crest of the ridge. Herrick allowed the weary bronc to keep its own pace then halted it close to the corpse. From the saddle, he took in the sign around the body.

It was a backshooting. The man had stopped two shots, Winchester shells to judge from the pair of holes in the back of the red flannel shirt and the bushwhacking was done from viciously close range. The man had been riding at the time; the sign of his mount was plain on the trail.

The killers, two of them, had holed up in the tangles of rock mere yards away, so the killing was an easy enough proposition. After it, the killers came out of hiding, mounted and leaving a plain story in the prints on the shaly page of the earth. After a close look at their victim, they rode off, leading his horse. They departed from the trail only a few yards from the body then went across the desert flats. That hard and waterless country was the doorstep of hell. Men had to know it before they traversed it.

Herrick stayed in the saddle, reflecting that this was no mere horse-thieving episode. The dead man was unlikely to have owned prime horseflesh. He was a nester, not a cowman. The woollen shirt, the faded blue bib-and-brace overalls, the heavy farmer's boots and the battered broad-brimmed straw hat, now on its crown in the dust, said so. Nester, sodbuster, plough-pusher, homesteader, he was one of a kind detested by free-range cattlemen.

Herrick left his saddle and strode into the rocks from which the killers had fired. It was ideal cover, this clutter of wind-eroded boulders. There was a sandy-floored area behind them. Herrick could see that the killers lay there, probably concealing their horses in more rocks behind them. They had peeked around the sheltering boulders, waiting for their victim to ride past. Then, just as he went by, he was bushwhacked from the rear. Herrick spent a long time studying certain marks in the dust indicative of the two who lay there. One, at least, had smoked three cigarettes, leaving their butts. He also left three dead matches and he had a peculiar habit when he'd lit his smoke.

He broke each match, snapping it almost in two.

Herrick next strode to the corpse for an examination. The buzzards had ravaged the exposed portions: the back of the head, the neck and the hands. He turned the body over. The face was middle-aged, already discoloured by death. The hair was greying and the body tolerably well fleshed and muscular. He had been a vigorous man and could have been a fighter, in contrast to the cattleman's stereotyped idea of the whining, hard-luck nester who busted decent cow grass with plough and spade.

In the pockets, Herrick found some loose change, a canvas bag of shag and a blackened pipe but nothing to identify him by name. The corpse was without side-arms and it was certain that, like most farmers, he hadn't carried a scabbard rifle. Fighter he might have been, but not with guns.

Herrick spent a sweaty half hour finding enough small rocks to cover the dead man under a cairn. He did not know what kind of law there was in Centro these days but he might find a way of having a coroner see the body of the sodbuster.

It was towards Centro that he rode after covering the body with the rocks, watched by the roosting buzzards, robbed of their carrion.

Something like a letter on the corpse might have given a clue as to the man's identity, he thought, and that made him think of the letter in his own back pocket — the one from Cal McDade which had brought him back to Arizona.

Herrick rode thoughtfully, but his eyes were always alert. He was 35 and the brand of the gunfighter was stamped on him. A Colt .45 rode, thonged down, at his thigh. His casual veneer covered the edginess of one who had lived by the gun for too long.

He hadn't seen this portion of Arizona Territory in a long time. It was a sprawl of spiny country within sight of the Dragoon Mountains. Not far to the east, beyond the arid flats, Tombstone town sweltered while, to the south, Arizona eventually became the state of Sonora in Mexico.

Herrick last rode here six years before, in the summer of 1881. The Earps were in Tombstone then and, in the fall of that year, Wyatt Earp and his droopy-moustached brothers had smoked out their grudge against the Clanton bunch at the OK Corral on Fermont Street. Now, the Earps were elsewhere; the Apaches and Yaquis had ceased to raid the settlements and homesteaders were drifting in to fence and plough the land. Herrick had seen their hard-scratch farms all along the frontier: sod shacks and structures of raw timber, surrounded by untidy yards with chickens and kids. And he had heard the dark mutterings of cowmen.

" . . . *Goddam government with its*

Homestead Act. We fought Injuns so we could run beef on open range, not have mealy-mouthed sodbusters string fences on it . . . "

Making a night-camp with a late spring round-up crew as he rode to the southwest, he heard one ugly boast: " *. . . we sure as hell run them nesters off, mister. To hell with claims filed away in Washington. This here is cow-country. We aim to keep it that way . . . "*

There were bitter voices to be heard in the scattered cowtowns, telling of a day coming when all cattlemen would have to fight for their free range. Herrick was a cattleman, too, a Texan whose father died for the Confederacy. When he heard of homesteaders coming in to fence the land under Washington-made law, it irked both cowman and Texan in him. But driving nesters off their claims by terror was something else again.

He had made a weary wayfaring from the northern ranges of Montana in this return to Arizona. They'd had a notorious winter up north. Already, it had earned a grotesque name. They called it 'The Big Die' from the numbers of cattle killed by the flesh-tearing winds. The brutal, pitiless blizzards turned half a million head into wolf-ravaged bones that northern winter of 1886 – 87. Cattlemen perished in the ceaseless white fury as they tried to save something of their herds. Families starved, ranches failed and gaunt, workless cowpokes took to the outlaw trial.

Some said it was a blow from which the cattle-raising business would never recover. There were those who felt there was truth in this gloomy prediction and Dan Herrick was among them. He had to admit that the crippling fact of The Big Die, coupled with the coming of the sodbusters, created a portent. Maybe it *was* true that the farmers would inherit the West, or at least enough of it to render the cowmen far less powerful. And where would men of Herrick's stamp be in an ordered society of farmers? He knew the answer well enough: they would be beyond the pale.

In the last few years, Herrick took the pay of frontier town councils to keep order on their streets using his gun, sanctioned by an oath and a tin star. Such sanctions only just kept some men on the right side of the law. Gunfighters with spotty reputations in one part of the frontier showed up elsewhere to be sworn in as peace officers. Mayors and councilmen had a way of turning a blind eye when they needed a speedy trigger behind their law badge.

Herrick was not of that breed but it was easy for him to be taken for such. He knew that respectable citizens might address him as 'Marshal' to his face but they privately viewed him as just another gun-heavy pariah and their wives drew their skirts aside when they passed on the plankwalks. He became tired of the dangerous life of overwork and meagre wages. Such honour as a marshal's post carried was scant and given grudgingly. There was also a deeper tiredness in him. Perhaps, with the foreshadowings of change in the land, he was beginning to outlive his time.

Had Elizabeth survived, marriage would doubtless have made him a citizen with roots. Maybe he'd have become stolid and paunchy, but he'd sure enough be happy. But Elizabeth had died and part of Dan Herrick died with her. So, he became a drifter. But, now, he was tired of it.

Perhaps he should have capitulated to the tiredness before now. When he reflected on what had overtaken the big-reputation gunfighters, he thought further about the changes so obviously coming. So many of the quick-trigger breed had written their brief legends of bullets and gunsmoke, then were felled by swifter or more cowardly guns. Others, like the swaggering Earps, found it healthier to make themselves scarce.

Herrick knew it was high time he quit. But he knew he could not quit as surely as he knew he was riding into trouble in returning to his old Arizona stamping ground. He came because the letter from Cal McDade caught up with him in the Montana town where he last held down the marshal's job. That McDade should write to him at all was a mystery for little love was lost between Herrick and the owner of the Walking C, where he had once been a top rider. Nevertheless, rip-roaring McDade would have been his father-in-law had Elizabeth lived. Not that the arrangement would have suited Cal McDade. He'd made it plain that no mere wrangler would marry his daughter. Equally, Dan Herrick insisted that Elizabeth would be his bride and, if the rancher refused to give her hand willingly, by God, he'd take her. After all, she was of age and had agreed to marry him. It would mean a start far

11

from her father's sphere of influence but they'd make it and be happy.

Then fate settled the argument. Laughing, dark-haired Elizabeth was carried away almost overnight in a shivering fever. When Herrick finally rode off Walking C grass, heavy-hearted and leaving Cal McDade grieving in his sprawling adobe ranch house, he thought he had seen the last of Arizona. Then came McDade's letter and its message was straight from the shoulder: McDade needed gunhands. Trouble was coming up and he figured the old Walking C might still mean something to Herrick. He was asked in so many words to throw his gun into the forthcoming fight, the precise nature of which remained unspecified.

So Dan Herrick returned to the tangled, sun-punished country, consciously setting up a guard against memories of Elizabeth which flooded back. But he knew it was her beloved memory which motivated him. He was not pushing his nose into this business — whatever it was — for Cal McDade's sake, but for Elizabeth's because her father seemed to be in trouble.

Centro was within easy reach now. There was little enough to the town; it was a desert-edge settlement of crumbling adobe buildings and weather-warped clapboard shacks. But Elizabeth slept in the red earth of its tiny cemetery. Typhoid carried her away so suddenly that, even now, all recollection of her death was a bad dream to Herrick. She was Cal McDade's only child, her mother having died giving birth to her 22 years before. If McDade and Herrick had anything in common it was that each in his particular way loved Elizabeth. A grinding bitterness as deep as Herrick's own settled into Cal McDade and a bleak gloom penetrated the Walking C. Herrick had waited until the bulk of the autumn work was through then asked for his time and rode north.

Now he was back, remembering as he

rode and thinking that the dead nester he found on the trail was an indication of trouble to come. Profoundly uneasy, he followed the trail around a hump of land from where it fell down to the desert edge and Centro. Away to his left, he made another discovery, spotting something which was not there when last he travelled this ridge. There was a forlorn scene down on the ridge-slope and he urged the bronc towards it to investigate.

It had been a homestead. Someone arrived here and built a homestead yard, surrounding a small shack and a barn. But someone else had arrived, bringing destruction. The yard fence was trampled flat, the shack was broken asunder, with only one wall remaining upright and the barn was partially torn down.

Herrick rode around the place slowly. He found evidence of a plough some distance beyond the ruined fence. Winter rains and snow had made mockery of the furrows and what remained of them was overgrown with catclaw and Spanish dagger. Dismounting to give the bronc a rest, he walked thoughtfully around what had been the yard. Weeds were now the only flourishing growths and tumbleweeds were jammed up against the surviving wall of the house. It must have been at least a year since the place was ravaged, he reasoned.

He remembered the boastful talk he heard when travelling, the talk of men who had run homesteaders off open range. He visualised men of his own kind, cattlemen, riding by night to terrorise nesters and destroy their efforts to create farms. Close to the wrecked house, he found the remains of a small doll in a tattered dress lying in the dust. He picked it up, looked at it then returned it with marked tenderness into the dust. In his mind stirred forgotten dreams about kids who might have been his and Elizabeth's if only she had survived.

He did not have to think long

15

about those who probably perpetrated this obscenity against some unknown family of hopeful nesters. This was free range across which he had often chased beef — Walking C beef. Of course, other stock also ran on this range, that of Dick Schultz's DS outfit and Charlie Costain's smaller Box-Bar. So, if McDade's riders were not the culprits, those of one of his neighbours were. Or maybe the whole bunch, acting in unison. He spat with disgust as he climbed back into the saddle.

All the way to Centro, he thought about the dead nester and the broken doll in the dust.

"There's bad medicine aplenty in this country, hoss," he said aloud. "A man'll be plumb lucky if it don't sooner or later poison him."

2

CENTRO had changed. It seemed to be even more sun-baked and much more seedy. The descending sun put a patina of glowing red on the clutter of adobe and plank buildings on either side of the rutted, single street. Crumbling and dusty, it looked as if had outlived its day, this settlement which had mushroomed with the cattle boom.

Herrick rode down the centre of the street, noting how empty the town was and he saw with a sense of shock that some familiar stores were now boarded up and derelict.

The headquarters of the Walking C could be reached without passing through Centro but memories drew Herrick back. Furthermore, he had been out of a real bed for too long and he needed to clean up. He hoped

Centro's Desert Palace Hotel was still functioning. Midway down the street, he purposely turned his eyes away from the high structure of Petersen's livery stable to prevent a particular memory from flowing back. It was after a summer hoe-down in the big barn behind Swede Petersen's place that Elizabeth said she would marry him. He walked on air that night, a stringy Texas wrangler with a few bucks saved who was out to marry the daughter of one of Arizona's smartest and richest cattlemen. Not that they would ride on Cal McDade's coat-tails when they were hitched. The carefully saved money amounted to a reasonable stake on a modest cow outfit in the Big Bend country of Texas. That was the couple's dream. But it crashed when typhoid came to the border country.

Even with his gaze turned away, the corner of his eye noted a bearded stranger lounging outside Petersen's place, looking as if he owned it. With renewed shock, Herrick thought that maybe friendly old Swede had sold out or was dead. Much could happen in six years.

Up ahead, however, some of the old Centro was left. Doc Grogan's office was still there; at least his name remained on its peeling false front. Tully's blacksmith's shop was there, too, as well as Miguel Chavez's cantina, favoured by the Mexican population.

Herrick remembered the spirit of the place six years back. Life on its only street fell quite a measure short of the bellowing, drunken and sinful excesses of Allen Street in Tombstone or Whiskey Row in Bisbee, but it had its moments. Newly paid cowpokes came hoorawing in for jags in the saloons, as did the miners from the already dwindling ore workings. There were fist fights and a shooting once in a while. But those were only the moments. Mostly, its long and boring hours were sleepy and fly-plagued and it was no better and no worse than other Arizona Territory border towns.

Sight of the warped wooden bulk of the Desert Palace Hotel at the far end of the street brought pleasurable anticipation of his easing away the grinding horseback miles in a hot bath and a halfway comfortable bed. There should be good feed and clean straw for his bronc in the hotel's stable, too. An overnight stay at the Desert Palace would give him a chance to show up at the Walking C rested, cleaned and shaven and that was a consideration of some importance. He once told Cal McDade he was going to marry his daughter and if he didn't like it he could go to hell. He strode away from the rancher's spluttering abuse walking tall.

Now, McDade had asked him to return and he aimed to do so looking unlike a saddle-tramp — and still walking tall.

Up ahead, he spotted activity on Centro's street. People and horses were clustered near the Desert Palace. They took shape out of the slanting rays of the setting sun: a knot of animals and big-hatted riders standing off to one side while a group of people was lined up on the opposite side of the street. Between the two groups were a couple of loaded buckboards.

A shrill voice rose and fell and Herrick saw that a young woman was haranguing those who sat on the buckboards. She was slender, wearing a calico dress and her golden hair was bonnetless. Her arms made dramatic gestures and the horsemen lined up near the hotel seemed to be amused. Her derisive voice carried on the dry evening air:

" . . . All right — quit! If you're so spineless, quit! But I'm not quitting, nor is my brother. I thought we were supposed to be standing together in this, but now that the intimidation is so strong, you're running for the brush like jackrabbits. Well, the rest of the jackrabbits out yonder are welcome to you!"

21

Her tirade was aimed at a couple of hangdog looking men, one at the reins of each buckboard. They had the homesteader look and their wives sat stolidly beside them. One couple, younger than the other, had two small boys aboard their wagons. Both buckboards were loaded with furniture and Herrick was reminded of the homesteader families he had seen moving in to take over their claims up north. Except this pair of families were obviously moving out and the slender, golden-haired girl was annoyed about it. He yanked leather and sat watching her.

Even with her brows drawn down in anger, she was pretty. She had high cheekbones and huge blue eyes which flashed with fire as she tore into the quitters.

"You're turning your backs on everything you've tried to begin building," she accused. "We're here legally and the law gives us every right to stay. If we stand together, we might find enough courage to lick these bullies."

She was plucky, thought Herrick. Plumb full of pluck and obviously pretty determined. This girl looked like the kind who would probably still be fighting even when she knew her cause was lost.

The elder of the men on the buckboards raised a thin-voiced excuse. "It's all very fine to talk about what's legal, Dorcas, but there ain't no law to back us up hereabouts. Leastways, not *real* law."

From among the halted riders off to one side, there came a harsh cackle of mocking laughter. These men deeply interested Dan Herrick and he constantly monitored them with a corner of his eye. There were five of them, in motley range gear. The way they wore their shell belts and holstered Colts told well enough what they were — border ruffians.

There was a sixth man, mounted a little apart from the rest and he was something else again. He was on a big chestnut in good trim and looked as if he was in command. His outfit was a mixture of black and grey and of the style favoured by preachers and gamblers. His vest was grey, so was the flat-crowned hat, set squarely on his head. His face was dark, with a black bar of moustache and his hair flowed from under his hat, carefully combed into a shoulder-length cascade in the mode of long-haired gunfighters who took Wild Bill Hickok as a model. It was black, but well streaked with silver. He was running to a paunch; this long-haired gunfighter was getting old. He was, nevertheless, dangerous. That might be deduced from the way he had his black frock-coat hitched back from the waist to show a broad belt of tooled leather and a holster holding a Navy Colt. It was tied down to his leg with a thong. His belt buckle was large and ornate and it particularly attracted Herrick's attention. It bore the head of a Texas longhorn, modelled in high relief, with silver horns protruding well forward.

This rider's face was totally impassive, but there was a menacing glitter in his dark eyes which was accentuated by the shadow of his hat-brim. And the eyes were fixed unwaveringly on Herrick.

Herrick kept the tail of his eye on the man. He couldn't put a name on him but knew that, when he heard it, it would be familiar. He was a stone cold professional gunfighter — someone with a reputation.

All the time, the girl in the calico dress dealt out her tongue-lashing with controlled anger. "Of course there's no real law. Nor will there be unless the likes of us stay around and make this end of the Territory respectable and fit for decent people to live in. Can't you see that we represent the future? We're working to make something of this land. These others have had their day. They're misusing the land and they're too greedy and violent to tolerate people who will do otherwise."

"Ain't no use shoutin', Dorcas," said the old man in his jittery voice. "We ain't fightin' people and we ain't stayin' here to be killed. Your talk won't amount to much when you're shot dead."

"That's right, Dorcas," put in the younger man. "Esther and me have two kids an' we've all tolerated enough misery since comin' here. We're willin' to admit it was a mistake to take up a homestead." He sounded utterly defeated but his wife, who had a genteel look out of place in the average homesteader, appeared ashamed and stared mutely at the ground.

"We better be movin'," piped up the older man. "We only stopped off in town for supplies for the journey. We'll have to push hard to reach the railhead at Benson before midnight."

The girl gave a mingled sigh of disgust and resignation.

Another snigger issued from the group of mounted men and Dorcas turned to face them angrily. It was then that she caught her first sight of Herrick. She looked at him hard and the fighting glow in the blue eyes intensified. "Look, another new drifter come to kill and grab whatever pickings he can," she said bitterly. "Well, he and all the others can hear what I have to say. They might run some folks out, but not Bob and me. We're staying — and we'll fight!"

Herrick reflected that his long journeying must have made him look downright unsavoury. No one had ever tagged him for border scum before.

But his admiration for the girl increased. She was slight, vulnerable and alone. Her own kind were sneaking away in the background, scared out of their wits and off to seek the safety of places like Chicago or St Louis. Still, she stood her ground with devil-be-damned determination.

Again, there was a cackle of amusement from among the riders, whom Herrick continued to keep in the corner of his view. He was interested in their horses. The professional gunfighter's animal was plainly his own property, but his companions were saddled on tough little cow-ponies, of the kind belonging to the remuda of any cattle outfit. One of them switched its tail against annoying flies and pranced around in an agitated way. Its flanks came into Merrick's view. He saw what he had almost expected to see but hoped he would not. There it was, however, unmistakable even in the dying rays of the sun — Cal McDade's Walking C brand.

From the midst of the riders came a hooting, lustful voice.

"Hey, girlie, if you want to fight, why not try fightin' me?"

Saddle gear creaked and a man came down from his mount, a squat man, powerfully built in the arms and chest. He had a blocky, double-chinned, leering face. He high-heeled across the rutted street, making for the girl while his companions yipped out rebel yells and growls of encouragement. All except the long-haired man in black and grey. He simply sat there, motionless, still more intent on Herrick than on anything going on around him.

"Try fightin' me!" bawled the squat man again. "The old fashioned way — no holds barred!" He reached Dorcas and prodded her breast.

Herrick came down from his saddle, sped across to the man in four loping strides, came behind him and grabbed his neckcloth. He yanked him backwards, causing him to spin around and he planted his right fist into his nose with a satisfying, squelchy thud.

The man staggered back, gurgling and with his arms waving madly. Herrick brought his fist down in a swift arc and drove it into the squat man's belly. The border ruffian gave a gusting belch of pain, his knees buckled and he staggered blindly, trying to keep his balance. Then he pitched forward into the dirt.

"The old fashioned way — no holds barred!" stated Herrick coldly.

There was a squawk from the knot of Walking C men. "By God! Look what he's done to Floyd! He can't get away with this!"

Horses pranced quickly and there was a move for which Dan Herrick was wholly prepared: a grabbing for holstered guns.

He whirled around and had the .45 naked in his hand before any of the riders cleared leather. Now, he was facing them, half-crouched in the gunfighter fashion. The .45 had moved from its holster into his hand without any of them seeing the draw and his eyes missed nothing, slithering menacingly from one gun-ruffian to the next. Each sat frozen, knowing the calibre of the man who held them under his gun muzzle.

"Don't try anythin'," he cautioned.

In this situation, the man in black and grey required special attention and Herrick kept aware of him. He remained motionless in his saddle, still watching Herrick with that glint of danger in his eye. At any moment, it might be translated into a gunfighter's response. Still, he sat there, stolid and silent.

Then, taking his time about it, he spoke. "One of you had better help Floyd up to his horse. He should have known better than to treat a lady that way. Behaviour of that kind is downright distasteful to behold." His silky voice betrayed some past other than that of carrying a gun on the frontier and he seemed to be genuinely fastidious. "Come on, let's have Floyd up on his feet."

He delivered orders as though in command, despite Herrick having the gunpoint advantage. All the time, he watched Herrick in that smouldering and calculating way. Herrick kept him warily in view, knowing that, under the distraction of movement, the professional might grab for that Navy Colt in the tied-down holster.

In the dirt of the street, Floyd was stirring and trying to get to his feet.

His face was bruised and his nose was running blood.

"Help Floyd up," repeated the long-haired one. "Put him on his horse and get him out of town. With your permission, of course, friend." A frosty smile appeared under the black moustache and the eyes still glittered menacingly towards Herrick.

Herrick held the gunfighter's pose while a couple of the riders dismounted to help Floyd. The departing homesteaders were already driving their buckboards down the street and the group of curious Centro citizenry in front of the Desert Palace had melted away like the snows of spring at the first suggestion of gun play on the street. Dorcas now looked utterly alone.

The long-haired man looked towards her and touched the brim of his hat.

"I'm sorry you had to endure such a display of bad manners, ma'am," he said in his silky way. "I'm afraid there are some who have never had the advantage of any exposure to etiquette.

Probably, it's only to be expected in a gopher-hole of a town such as this. On the whole, a lady like yourself might be better advised to seek a more civilised atmosphere." It had a sincere enough ring but it carried a barb in the suggestion that Dorcas, too, should leave these parts.

Tension climbed as Herrick retained his gunfighting stance. Two or three of the men on Walking C cow-ponies might clear leather, but they had witnessed Herrick's eye-defying draw and were not taking any risks. Any man who could draw that fast must surely be equally handy with the trigger. He might drop a number of them before anyone dropped him.

With Floyd back in his saddle, the long-haired man danced his big chestnut forward a few paces and fixed Herrick with his brightly smouldering gaze.

"We'll meet again, friend," he promised smoothly. "In the not-too-distant future, I hope." His mouth

33

worked itself into a curl of contempt.

He danced his horse around, placed himself at the head of the group of riders and indicated with a commanding jerk of his head that they should follow him. The bunch wheeled behind him and pounded off along the street in the direction which would lead to the Walking C holdings.

Dan Herrick slowly unwound from his crouch as the riders went into the gathering shadows. He holstered his Colt and stepped towards his bronc. Dorcas approached him slowly and shyly. With her prettiness and her shapeliness within the simple calico dress, she reminded him of Elizabeth. She seemed lost for words, but gave him a quiet smile. Herrick touched the brim of his hat to her, took the leathers of his animal in hand and walked it towards the alleyway behind the Desert Palace. There was a reasonably well equipped stable belonging to the hotel back there in the old days, he recalled.

Just before entering the alley, he looked back towards the knot of Walking C riders, now bulking darkly in the shadow distance of the street.

He was thinking of the long-haired man in black and grey and of his promise that they would meet again.

"We sure will, mister," he muttered.

For the long-haired one's parting comment was underpinned by a more eloquent but wordless exchange in a currency universal among gunfighters. It was done through a locking of smouldering looks. Through it, a challenge was made and accepted but each man had signalled his willingness to bide his time.

Eventually, it would come to a sixgun showdown between these two. And only one would remain alive when the sixguns fell silent.

3

THE stable at the rear of the hotel was still there, guarded by a youngster.

"Brush him down, water him, feed him and give him some bedding," Herrick told the kid, handing over the bronc's leathers and fishing a quarter from his pocket. "I'm staying at the hotel for the night." He guessed he wasn't being presumptuous on that point. There was a time when the Desert Palace frowned on mere punchers but it looked as if things in Centro had changed to the degree where the hotel would welcome anyone capable of paying his bill.

Hearing a light footfall at the stable door, he turned with instinctive speed. Dorcas stood there. In spite of her recent tough talk to the quitting nesters, she now looked vulnerable, like a lost little girl. She walked closer to Herrick and said: "If you're staying around here for long, watch out for those men. Particularly the fancy one with the long hair. He's dangerous."

"I know it," said Herrick. "Thanks for the warning, though."

"I want to thank you — and apologise."

"That's all right." Herrick felt acute embarrassment.

"They might easily have killed you and would have done it if they managed to draw their guns. They're that kind. I thought you were the same kind. That's what I want to apologise for."

Herrick gave a wry smile. "Well, it's a considerable comfort to know you don't have me tagged with those fellows, ma'am, and I thank you for your kindness," he said. "As for killin' me, well I guess they just didn't get a chance to draw their guns."

He swung his warsack over his shoulder and made for the stable door. The girl walked beside him.

The prospect of food, a hot bath and a bed was alluring but there were many questions in his mind concerning this place where a man lay bushwhacked, where gun-heavy rannihans rode horseflesh bearing a once honoured brand and where homesteaders were running scared.

"Those gents have some folk pretty well over a barrel, don't they?" he asked.

"Yes, and it's getting worse. I'm as scared as anyone else, but I meant what I said about standing and fighting. And that goes for my brother, Bob, too."

"I figure there's no mistakin' your determination. Look, is there any place you and I can talk? I'd like to know more about what goes on around here."

They were out of the alley and on the street now, heading for the front gallery of the hotel. Dorcas indicated a lamp-yellowed window on the far side of the street. "That's a restaurant yonder, with my buckboard hitched outside. It's not much of a place but it's usually quiet. We can talk there."

"Fine, I'm hungry anyway. You go ahead and I'll join you there when I've checked in at the hotel."

He halted before the Desert Palace and watched her cross the street, mount the far plankwalk and enter the eating house. Humping his warsack up the gallery steps, he thought of the men mounted on animals branded with the Walking C. What had happened to the old crew? Hard cases with bunkhouses in the old days. Cal McDade had been a youthful major with Hood's Texans in the big war and he selected his men with an officer's eye. There must have been some big changes in the Walking C and in McDade, too.

Herrick's mouth quirked into another wry smile as he walked into the Desert Palace. For the hotel, too, brought memories of the old Walking C men. Rough and ready but great-hearted and top hands at their game, they were the best of companions to side you in any kind of ruckus. Men like Shorty Billings, the foreman; Tex Odell, Frenchy Gascoine, Sam Ames and the rest would hardly share coffee and beans with the riff-raff he had encountered on Centro's street. But everything had changed hereabouts.

The once-elegant Desert Palace had changed as well. Its gilded fittings were peeling and showing themselves for the elaborate fakes they were, the carpets were worn and the whole place was dusty and shabby. It was empty, too, save for a pimply youth who eyed Herrick from behind the reception desk. There was no sign now of the hearty, prosperous cattlemen, the mining engineers, the slick-suited liquor and dry goods drummers and the Eastern visitors with their fashionable wives who once thronged the place.

Herrick figured to-day's Desert Palace would not scorn a mere wrangler's patronage and he was right. The pimply youth suddenly looked lively, even if he did seem to feel the new arrival was another gunnie who had drifted into the locality. "Can I help you, sir?" he asked. Herrick dumped his warsack on the floor in front of the desk.

"Sure. I'm lookin' for a room for to-night and maybe a bath."

"Very good, sir. There's number twenty-six. Very convenient for the bathroom at the end of the corridor, too." The youth took a key from the board behind him. "I'll show you the way."

He walked towards the wide stairway and Herrick followed him, trying to keep a straight face but recalling the Desert Palace's earlier snooty staff. Recalling, too, the time Frenchy Gascoine got drunk and barged into the hotel to do a little hell-raising. Tex Odell, Sam Ames and Herrick went in after him to restrain him and save the good name of the Walking C. Since they'd all been imbibing, a good-natured brawl ensued. A potted palm was damaged, a window was broken and nervous guests took refuge behind the furniture, fearing that the lawless

41

cowboys were about to shoot the place to splinters.

Cal McDade, who had been conferring with meat market men from Chicago in a back room, showed up to soothe the manager who was yelling for the town marshal. He declared he didn't know why the man was bellyaching and, if he'd been in Hays or Dodge in the old days when the first Texas herds arrived, he would have seen real rowdy punchers on the rampage. The rancher cheerfully agreed to pay for the damage and Herrick, Frenchy, Tex and Sam left with their arms around each other, raising four of the most woeful voices in Arizona Territory in "I'm A-ridin' Old Paint."

Now, he was back in a Desert Palace which was clearly running to seed but the room was clean and the bed looked comfortable. He told the youth he would be back in about an hour and the youngster said he would arrange for the bath to be ready.

Herrick crossed the street and found

Dorcas at a corner table of the eating house with a cup of coffee before her. The place was empty of customers save for her. The yellow lamplight put highlights into her golden hair and emphasised the softly sculptured planes of her face. She gave him a shy smile and, once again, he was reminded of Elizabeth. They introduced themselves. The girl's surname was Holbrook.

He could not remember this restaurant from the old days and supposed it opened after he left. Like everything else in town, it appeared to be on the downgrade. A lugubrious man in a greasy apron emerged from behind the counter and Herrick interpreted his raised eyebrow as a request for his order. He took beans, sausage, bread and coffee. Dorcas settled for another cup of coffee.

The food was surprisingly good and he began to eat rapidly, gulping coffee at intervals. Then he remembered the presence of the girl and self-consciously mended his manners. Dorcas watched, smiling slightly. He mumbled an apology adding: "I'm all-fired hungry, I guess."

"Go ahead and enjoy it," said Dorcas. "You seem to be hungry and tired. You must have been riding for a long time."

"I came from a long ways up north," he answered. He took a sip of coffee and weighed his next words, wondering how she would take them. "I came to see Cal McDade."

The hint of amusement faded from her eyes. "Not to ride for him?"

Herrick shrugged. "Just to see him. I rode for him a long time ago but from what I'm learnin' he's not the man he was then. I still want to see him. I have questions for him."

"I don't know what kind of man he used to be, but I know what he is now," she said coldly. "He's mean and vicious. He believes he can bully homesteaders off the land, using the ruffians you saw out there. He thinks he can still run cattle on land the government plainly say is ceded over to us under the Homesteader Act. It's our land, the kind of land my brother Bob and I are trying to shape up into a farm."

"I guess he knows well enough it's against the law to run beef on homestead claims but it's federal law and there are some aspects of that kind of law which will never suit old rebels like McDade," mused Herrick. "They got in here first after the big war and made things go their way."

"But President Arthur said he'd clean up Arizona even if he had to send federal troops to settle the lawless elements. It never happened around here but some day it will. This pocket of the territory might hold out for a while but, one day, we'll have real law officers instead of that wretched old man Yawberry who's supposed to be town marshal in Centro."

"Dick Yawberry? Is he still around?" Herrick asked, surprised. "He must be over seventy by now?"

"He's old, all right. And he's a

drunk. He's also in McDade's pocket and he has a couple of deputies who might just as well be McDade hands." Dorcas said scornfully.

Herrick pushed his empty cup around the table thoughtfully. So old Dick Yawberry was still around here and there was probably still not a US Marshal closer than Tucson. True, President Chester Arthur had declared he would have lawlessness rooted out of Arizona Territory as a reaction to the goings-on in Cochise County in the days of the Earps and Clantons and the hangers-on to both factions. But this was always a forgotten end of the Territory and things had obviously not changed. He could see that, with McDade making a last ditch stand for the old hell-roaring order, this would become a final haven for border scum as the rest of the West tamed itself.

"Seems to me you homesteaders should go to Tucson and talk to the authorities," he told the girl.

"We considered that," she, said.

"And one of us talked too much about it. A young fellow named Sam Rogerson. He was single and working a place on his own. We talked about getting federal law and forming a protection group for the homesteaders. He came into Centro to do a little drinking once in a while and I guess that was his weakness. Afterward, we thought he must have talked too much in one of the saloons."

"Afterward?"

"After he was found lying outside his shack — shot dead."

Herrick had a vivid vision of the corpse he found in the desert dust, now lying under the stone cairn. So there was an earlier killing. Better hold his tongue about the dead nester he found, however. There was no point in scaring Dorcas any further, she'd had enough emotional upheavals for one day.

The man in the greasy apron appeared with the coffee pot and poured more for both customers. Herrick kept silent until he had finished and retreated to his kitchen.

"Walking C's work?" he asked.

"You can be sure it was done by McDade's gunhands," she answered bitterly. "Homesteaders are running out all the time because of them but, if just enough stay to eventually start fighting back, we might keep what's legally ours. We will if my brother Bob has his way. He's trying to carry on Sam Rogerson's ideas. They were sound enough in spite of Sam being loose-tongued about them. Bob wants the homesteaders to form their own protection group. There are a few who might still make a stand if encouraged."

Herrick saw determination in her eyes, as if thought of her brother stiffened her resolve to stand and fight. This Bob must be an inspiring influence; he hoped he was capable of giving the nesters the confidence he gave his sister. If enough nesters remained around, that was.

He was suddenly surprised at his own train of thought. At rock bottom, he was a cowman but here he was, siding with sodbusters who, in the cowman's view, intruded upon good graze to bring it under the plough. All his cattleman's sensitivities kicked against the notion of open range becoming farmland but the ravaged homestead returned to his memory, quickly followed by recollection of the bushwhacked nester, the Walking C gunnies on the street and the newly imparted word of an earlier bushwhacking. Then came the memory of McDade's letter in his pocket.

McDade wanted him to return to Arizona because he had an offer to make. Herrick had already received an insight into the kind of play McDade made these days, but he had to follow up that letter and ride to Walking C headquarters. Some strong force impelled him even though he knew that, after his run-in with the gun-ruffians, Walking C grass would

49

be dangerous territory. It would be a chore for to-morrow, after a good night's sleep.

They finished their coffee. Herrick paid for their orders and they returned to the street which was now dark. They walked to Dorcas's hitched buckboard and he helped her up to the seat.

As she gathered up the reins, Dorcas looked down at him, her face shrouded by the night. "Thank you for everything," she said. The shy smile came again. Herrick merely touched the brim of his hat.

Dorcas slapped the leathers against the horse's flanks and the buckboard trundled away. Herrick stood in the middle of the street, watching the vehicle until it and the lonely girl were gathered into the darkness.

In the room at the Desert Palace, he slept like a dead man and made an early start in the morning. The lugubrious owner of the eating house was hardly awake when Herrick troubled him for ham, eggs and coffee and there was still not a soul on the street when he rode out of town.

The sun was climbing to 11 o'clock when he brought the bronc down the slanting land to the bed of the Santa Clara Sink. The water bubbled as good as ever down in the scrub-protected spring where someone — probably the Spanish adventurers who once claimed this land for Spain — made a rock-lined basin to hold the gift which spouted from the earth. Out of the great mother earth was how the Indians who had claimed the land even earlier would have put it. Yet it was not quite a claim. For the Apaches, whose stronghold this region was before the defeat of Geronimo, had no concept of land as property. Their lives were tuned to the pulse of the great earth; they did not try to master the land under a yoke of ownership. They venerated the land and it rewarded them.

Not a bad way of looking at things, he thought. He walked the animal to the water, allowed it to drink then, at an outgrowth of scrub, hitched it to a stout branch. Returning to the water, he drank noisily.

This spring, at the bottom of a deep basin, was a compellingly beautiful oasis. Elizabeth loved to ride to the Santa Clara Sink for, whoever claimed it through history, it was now on Walking C land. Its strong mystic spirit appealed to Elizabeth, a true daughter of the Southwest. Possibly, something there was attuned to her soul, just as it was to those of the Indians. But, if anything of her lingered here now, it was surely good and beneficial, where Indian lore declared that the spirits left by the dead were frequently evil and malignant, no matter how noble their owners in life.

Walking the bronc around the water, Herrick mounted and rode up the other side of the basin. Near its rim, he looked back, remembering how Elizabeth and he once sat beside the water, making plans.

His lapse into sentiment caused him

to be caught off guard.

Just as he reached the top of the basin, two riders appeared over it. They halted their mounts full in his path and looked down at him. They controlled their animals with their knees for their hands were fully occupied — holding Winchester repeaters, levelled plumb at Herrick's face.

His right hand moved but was stilled by the menacing jerk of a Winchester barrel.

"Don't go for your iron or you'll have no head under your hat," warned a grating and gloating voice.

It was that of Floyd, the gun ruffian whom Herrick had whipped in Centro the day before. And it dripped with gleeful anticipation of brutal revenge.

4

FLOYD'S face was swollen and severely bruised but he grinned in triumph. It would not take much to make him trigger the Winchester.

His partner was a thin, worn-down oldster with a mournful oxbow of moustache under a beaky nose. Herrick remembered him from the Walking C bunch of the previous day. Doubtless some displaced wrangler from the north, he looked as if the icy miseries of The Big Die lingered in his old bones. But his eyes were dangerous.

"Better hold still and tell us what you're doin' on Walking C grass," growled Floyd.

"None of your damned business," responded Herrick.

Floyd's horse suddenly shook its head and, with a jingle of ringbits, the oldster's mount pranced a couple of steps, raising its upper lip impatiently, but the Winchesters remained steadily levelled.

Herrick read the sign. The pair were above him, within sight of the water, down at the sink. The fractious shifting of the horses was a reaction to its nearness. Probably, the two Walking C gunhands spotted his approach from the far side of the basin, maybe from concealment in the brush. Their animals had scented the water long before reaching it. Now, it tantalised them and they were eager to drink.

Mere yards separated the Walking C pair from Herrick. He had blundered right into their hands and they had the drop on him at close range. He cursed himself as a damn fool because, in the face of those bleak facts, he had given them an answer which heightened their eagerness to kill him. Had he responded to their challenge by saying he was there because Cal McDade sent for him, use of their boss's name might easily have guaranteed free passage.

As it was, they meant deadly business. Blood lust smouldered in their eyes. Floyd wanted raw revenge and the oldtimer was set on sheer vicious participation.

"Yes, sir, this is your reckoning day," hissed Floyd. "Now we know who you are, we'll ride you off a ways before we shoot you as an armed trespasser. Wouldn't be fittin' to leave your carcase around here. Buzzards is ugly things to have flappin' around good water."

At that moment, another spasm of jittery twitching caused Floyd's mount to fling its head to one side and prance backwards. The split instant gave Herrick his chance.

His hand, still held in a frozen claw, almost brushing the butt of his Colt, streaked down. It came up in a swift arc, with the gun bucking and slamming a brief rope of flame into Floyd's chunky body. At the same time, Herrick made a lightning but controlled ducking action, swinging the .45 towards the oldster and loosing another shot. The oldtimer heaved violently backwards in his saddle with a look of total surprise printed on his face. He blasted a shot with a dying hand, sending a shell screaming through space which Herrick had occupied a moment before, and a Winchester report clattering off over the wide land.

Herrick's bronc fiddlefooted nervously in a fog of gunsmoke as Herrick righted himself in the saddle. Floyd's body was still saddled, hairpinned forward from the waist with the head and arms dangling at one side of his horse's neck. His undischarged Winchester lay on the ground. The oldster had cleared his stirrups with a dying kick and his body had slithered to the ground where it lay like a crumpled bag of bones.

Herrick spat the acid taste of gunsmoke from his mouth and gave a shudder of self-disgust. It had been self defence, the Walking C pair having declared the plain intention of killing him. He had killed before, strictly as a law officer, but the act of taking a man's life always brought stomach churnings of self-contempt.

There was added chagrin in having killed here, in this place which Elizabeth had loved.

What was that word the Navajo had for the ghosts which they believed lurked on after death? *Chindi*. Well, he thought, if there was any *chindi* of Elizabeth lingering at the Santa Clara Sink, he hoped it was not too ashamed of him. On the other hand, maybe it was Elizabeth's good ghost which, guardian angel like, had saved him from the murderous pair. For, while Navajo *chindi* were always malevolent, any shade of Elizabeth could only be good. Perhaps her influence would dispel the wretched shades of the two gun-ruffians from this wholesome place, too.

It was a hell of a way for a man to be thinking — like an Indian, steeped in an ancient lifeway which the white man claimed to have replaced with his own allegedly civilising influence, he reflected. But love of Elizabeth would always live in him and she had treasured this land and all its legends.

He heeded Floyd's observation about having buzzards flapping around good water, dismounted and walked the pair's horses back over the lip of the basin, leaving Floyd's corpse still a-saddle. He left the body in a clump of brush, walked towards the sink, recovered the Winchesters and thrust them back in their saddle-scabbards, then looped the leathers of the horse around their saddle horns. He left the animals to graze, knowing they would make for the water, drink, then head back by instinct towards the Walking C headquarters. Lastly, he hauled the body of the stringy oldster to the brush clump and stretched it beside that of Floyd.

He rode stolidly onward, knowing that the arrival of the two riderless horses would alert the Walking C to the fate of the two gunnies. By that time, he hoped to have finished his visit to Cal McDade. For having come this far, he aimed to continue and find out from McDade himself why he had been sent for and exactly where McDade, hitherto a tough but undeniably fair man, stood in the dirty game of nester persecution.

He knew that the Walking C horses would take their time about it, browsing on the land and walking at slow, unridden pace, but those two corpses in his backtrail could have a slow-fuse effect. Once the Walking C had word of the killings at the sink, he could be corked up in the midst of hostile men.

Herrick wondered about the presence of Floyd and his companion where he had encountered them, out on the fringe of McDade's holdings. He wondered if McDade had posted lookouts at points across his land. He had known such a situation before, as in the Murphy-Chisum range war in New Mexico, in which a stranger ventured on to the land of either faction at his peril.

Eventually, through slitted eyes, he caught sight of two riders on a far rise. They wavered deceptively in the heat haze but he guessed they were sitting still, watching his approach. They moved more perceptively and were clearly coming down the rise towards him. He nudged his Colt loose in its holster.

Herrick maintained his mount's steady pace and the Walking C riders approached at a brisker pace. Slowly, from a pair of blobs, they became a couple of seedy saddle tramps, two more of the border ruffian type. With eyes scrunched against the sun, Herrick considered them as the dwindling distance revealed them in more detail. He figured he had seen them the previous day, among the bunch who had taunted Dorcas in Centro. They were thin, flat-bellied specimens, with faces burned black by the sun. They had sixguns holstered in their scuffed shellbelts and the conspicuous way they kept their hands away from their weapons made Herrick feel they remembered him, too, and his lightning draw in the Centro run-in.

Caution was obvious in their approach as they pulled rein in front of him. They were supposedly guarding this land and tried to act as if they were. Nevertheless, they were the no-account kind with no great gift of courage. Herrick could be dangerous.

Trying to sound important, one rasped: "Where you headed, pilgrim?"

Herrick yanked rein. This time, he would play it differently.

"Walking C. I have business with Major McDade." He leaned easily in his saddle and lifted an eyebrow, as if requesting the next question.

Showing increased caution, the man asked it. "What do you want with the Major?"

"Business. Personal business. He

62

wrote me and asked me to call on him." He stated it in a tone which implied that he would tell them nothing more. Mention of McDade's name had disarmed them. They were taking no chances with a man they knew to be a swift gunhand to whom McDade had sent a written request. Chances were he was someone extra special whom the major wanted in on his end of the fight.

"We heard three shots back yonder," said the second gunnie, changing the subject.

That answered a question which had lurked in Herrick's brain since the gunplay at the sink. He had wondered if there was anyone within earshot who might be alerted by the shooting. Now, he hoped that distance had thinned the sound sufficiently to disguise the fact that one report was that of a Winchester.

"That was me, killing a rattler. Damn varmint was coiled up right in front of my cayuse and it spooked him. Had to put three slugs into him. You know how darned stubborn rattlers can be."

"Sure," said the rider. But suspicion remained on the faces of the pair.

"You see anythin' of a couple of jaspers yonder?" asked the man who had opened the questioning.

"Yeah, a gentleman I believe I had the pleasure of meeting yesterday and an elderly gent. We exchanged the time of day."

"Uh-huh," grunted the rider. "I figure it's all right for you to go ahead."

Herrick guessed that these sentinels now believed he had satisfied Floyd and his companion in their questionings and they had allowed him to proceed. Maybe they had even swallowed his yarn about the rattler. At all events, they were not minded to hinder one specifically summoned by McDade, especially one whose speedy gunhand they had witnessed.

He reined the bronc forward and, after two minutes, turned and saw them watching him from still halted horses. No, all their suspicions were not yet dispelled.

He was now acutely aware that he was deep into Walking C territory — with two tell-tale corpses in his backtrail.

At length, he came to the Walking C headquarters and saw at once how much the place had changed as he approached the great arched gate of sapling poles at the entrance to the ranch yard.

The long adobe ranch house, with its Spanish style gallery, was more sun-raddled now and the attractive show of trailer roses which Elizabeth had once cultivated along the gallery front was gone. The barns were now sun-split and slanted and the roof of one sagged like an old sway-backed horse. The peeled pole corrals wherein he had once helped to dehorn snorty steers looked slovenly, with fallen poles lying around on the ground. The bunkhouse needed painting and even the stone watering trough, plumb centre of the yard, was crumbling.

Herrick felt the tug at his guts which always came when he thought of Elizabeth. The key to what was wrong with the place lay in the absence of the gallery roses: Elizabeth was gone. The touch of a gentle girl who loved orderliness and beauty had disappeared.

If an absence lay at the heart of the ramshackle appearance of the ranch, there were additions which emphasised how far the place had slid from its earlier status. They were the gun-heavy personages loafing around the yard. Three squatted on their heels, Texas style, over by one of the barns. Two more were smoking beside a woebegone corral. All were owlhooters of a kind Cal McDade would have hazed off the place in the old days. Except one.

Characteristically, he stood alone, close to one end of the gallery of the house, looking elegant, even in his lounging attitude. He was the long-haired professional, making his Navy Colt obvious and with the sun glittering on the longhorn belt buckle which so interested Herrick. He considered the newcomer with the same smouldering stare of the day before.

Herrick dismounted at the trough, watered his bronc then hitched it at the rack beside the trough, making his actions deliberate and all the time with his eyes on the long-haired one who continued to return the stare in his impassive way. He walked towards the gallery, feeling the eyes of the border ruffians in the yard on him. As he approached the steps, a figure emerged from the door of the house and a greeting was directed to him.

"By God, it's Dan! High time you showed up!"

The voice was thinner now and lacked the old fire which had blazed out of Cal McDade in the old days when he was a hell-roarer, heading a cow-crew known the length and breadth of Arizona Territory. He was dressed as Herrick always remembered him, in a rough work shirt, a buckskin vest, old jeans and cut-down riding boots with big rowelled Texas spurs. He wore a holstered Colt .45, as he always did, even inside his home. Habits learned in those days of the first Texas trail herds right after the Civil War and in the years of warring with the Apaches here in Arizona were engrained in Cal McDade.

When he came down the gallery steps, Herrick could see how stooped he had become. His face was drawn, too, and his spiky longhorn moustache was almost white where it had once the colour of rich snuff.

"It's good to see you, Dan," hailed the rancher, extending a tough hand. There was heartiness in this newer yet so much older McDade which he had never displayed before. Herrick saw at once that it was forced. The rancher was almost like a man welcoming home a long-lost son.

Briefly, Herrick wondered why he had come out to the Walking C headquarters. Events in Centro and the story told by Dorcas indicated well enough that there was a new game with a new deck of cards being played on these ranges. He wanted no part of it.

Deep down, however, he knew he was here because of Elizabeth. She was always a caring daughter. Even if things had worked out differently with Herrick and she, Elizabeth would have continued to be concerned about the old man and kept contact with him. Herrick would not have begrudged it. It was not just the letter from McDade which impelled him to continue his mission to the Walking C. Somehow, for Elizabeth's sake, he had to know how the rancher was faring.

It was no use telling himself he wanted no part of what was going on hereabouts. He had already taken a hand in it. He had made a play by shooting the pair at the Santa Clara Sink. Sooner or later, he would be forced to back up that play.

Meantime, here was Cal McDade, who had once declared that he was not good enough for his daughter, greeting him with noisy heartiness even though it was transparently false. Herrick had the feeling that it was all a show for the benefit of the gun-hung border drifters in the ranch yard.

"Come on into the house, Dan," said McDade. 'I heard tell there was a stranger in town who got into a ruckus with some of my men. It sounded like you." He chuckled but it was a piece of bad acting and carried no conviction. "Sounded like the old days when we had the old bunch here. Remember, how they'd put up some kind of high spirited show every time they hit town? Remember Frenchy's big hooraw at the Desert Palace? Frenchy moved on, y'know. Heard he married a girl from 'Frisco."

They walked up the steps and crossed the gallery with McDade still talking. "Remember the time Shorty Billings tried to fight three miners with only a beer bottle? Hah, Shorty was hard to hold when he was drunk. He was one fine foreman, though, the very best. Shorty moved on, too, went up to Nebraska. They all moved on."

"I figured that was the case. There's a whole bunch of new faces," commented Herrick drily.

McDade took him into the big living room. At once, he was assailed by memories of the girl he had loved to the extent that he scarcely noticed the lean, middle-aged man in range-garb who stood beside the table in the act of closing a large ledger. He could almost see Elizabeth moving around this room, the graceful and smiling hostess on the days when her father brought the whole crew in for food and drink. Christmas and Thanksgiving were happy times within these walls.

The memory of Elizabeth was here but nothing of her neat hand. The pair of longhorns mounted over the wide fieldstone fireplace had dropped

71

askew; pictures were slanted on the walls and there was dust everywhere. The huge picture window, divided into many smaller panes by a criss-crossing of wooden frames, needed cleaning.

Cal McDade inclined his head towards the man at the table.

"Dan, this here is my foreman, Ed Terry. He's new here since your time. Ed's a good man who sure knows the cattle business."

Ed Terry nodded a greeting towards Herrick. There was a precise neatness to his range gear. He had thin, thoughtful features and was obviously an intelligent man of different stamp from the ruffians who made up the ranch crew. There was an aloof quality to him and Herrick did not remember seeing him among the men he met the previous day.

Terry fished in the pocket of his shirt and produced the cigarette makings of Bull Durham tobacco and papers. He offered them to Herrick, asking: "Smoke?"

Herrick, who had never developed the habit, shook his head. Terry, knowing that McDade was a pipe smoker, did not offer the makings to the rancher. He leaned against the table, rolling a smoke with one hand and tapping the ledger with the other. Obviously, he and McDade were discussing business which was interrupted when McDade spotted Herrick crossing the yard, the door of the room giving a view across the gallery where the big window looked out at one side of the house.

"As I was saying, Major, that's how things stand at the present tally," he said. He produced a match and struck it on the coarse seat of his pants.

"Well, we're keepin' afloat at least," grunted McDade. "We've had better figures, but we're probably as healthy as we can expect to be in these damn peculiar times. Thanks, Ed. You won't mind if Dan here and I have a private chat?"

"Not at all, Major," said Terry

around the cigarette which he was in the act of lighting. He blew out the match and tossed it towards the fieldstone fireplace. With a parting nod to Herrick, he walked out on to the gallery.

"Ed's quite a find," said McDade. "I was lucky to find him after Shorty left. He had some years at the shipping end of the business with an uncle in Kansas City, so he sure knows beef. Betwixt you an' me, he's one of the few men around here I can really trust."

Herrick gave a non-committal grunt. He was looking at the spent match which Ed Terry had tossed at the fireplace.

It had missed the wide, empty grate under the big chimney and landed in the hearthstone. Before throwing it away, Terry had snapped it between two fingers and it lay there, making a perfect letter 'V', an exact replica of the matches Herrick found behind the rock which had sheltered the two bushwhackers.

McDade moved to an ornately carved cabinet in a corner and produced a bottle of Old Crow and two glasses. He poured two good measures.

"Glad you finally arrived, Dan. Fact is, I need a man of your calibre." As the glass was handed to him, Herrick noticed that the rancher's hand was shaking. He noticed, too, for the first time, that there was something almost pathetic in the old man's over-friendliness. With all his strained heartiness, he was like a drowning man clutching at a straw.

Herrick took the glass and sipped the liquor, thinking that the tremor was not confined to McDade's hand. Probably, he was shaking right inside his guts. Cal McDade was a tough product of tough times but, right at this moment, he was not far from being just a scared old man. Scared enough to have sent for Herrick when there was no love lost between them and greet him with a barrage of uncharacteristic friendly bluster.

"Your letter mentioned a big fight coming up," commented Herrick innocently. "What exactly did it mean?"

McDade killed off his liquor with a backward jerk of his head and sighed harshly as it grabbed at the lining of throat.

"Nester trouble," he said equally harshly. "Damned homesteaders in this region of the Territory. Before we know it, they'll have every last acre of halfway decent rangeland fenced and ploughed under."

Herrick now saw something else that was new in McDade: a tight bitterness in the lines of his face and a near fanatical glitter in his eyes. He had obviously developed a blazing hatred of homesteaders.

Herrick took another sip of the Old Crow and said thoughtfully: "Homesteading is legal when it's done properly under the Homestead Act and when it's on land designated as being in the public domain. That's the law."

"Law!" spluttered McDade. "Damned

76

Washington-made law, created by a bunch of Yankees! Law that favours their own blasted kind. Know what these nesters pay for a claim? Ten dollars — *ten* measly Yankee dollars! That gives them the right to fence off and plough land better men fought the Indians for. And do you know who's banned from takin' up a claim? Ex-Confederates! Anyone who fought for the South in what the Washington gang is pleased to call 'the great rebellion' can't benefit from the dubious favours of the Yankee government — not that any respectable Southerner, man or woman, would want to."

The rancher brushed back his big moustache and the fanatic glitter in his eyes intensified. "Well, I'm an ex-Confederate an' I'll be proud of it until I draw my last breath. Nobody made me into an artificial Yankee at war's end. I came into this country with hardly a pair of pants an' fought the Apaches to build up this spread. Now that the real men have done the hard work, the blamed plough-pushers are in here on ten-dollar claims. Well, they and the ones that made it easy for them to come in never took a chance on havin' an Apache lance shoved through their guts. So why should my kind tolerate 'em?"

Herrick knew well enough what was at the root of McDade's violent objection to the homesteaders. It was the same as that of ranchers all over the country. For years, they ran cattle on land to which they had no legal right or title, public land which they had claimed only by conquest. But their reign was rapidly drawing to an end.

As Herrick finished his whisky, McDade claimed his glass. Pouring two refills, his hand shook so violently with anger that the bottle chattered against the rims of the glasses. It was clear that the rancher had built up a mental picture of the homesteaders as a threat of ogre-like proportions, powered by the machinations of the United States government in Washington. Herrick wondered if maybe the old man had not become a little unbalanced.

"So you're filling up the Walking C with gents like those outside to meet the challenge and you figure I'd help out?" he asked.

"Sure, somethin' like that," replied McDade. His spluttering indignation gave way to a more confidential tone. "Y'see, these hands I have workin' for me, — well, I'd like to have one among 'em who could be trusted . . . "

His words petered out but, stumbling as they were, they were eloquent enough for Herrick. They revealed the situation at the Walking C plainly enough and Herrick knew why the rancher was so jittery.

The 'hands', as he called them, could prove dangerous to McDade himself. The real hands, the good Walking C men of old, were gone and, in collecting a bunch of border hardcases, McDade had a tiger by the tail. It had happened before. Take the Lincoln County War, over in New Mexico, not too long ago. The men whose concern was land and property, the Murphys and McSweens, could hardly have known what they were getting into when they brought in gunpacking riders to do their fighting. In no time at all, the mercenaries were calling the play. Men like Tom O'Phalliard, Dave Rudabaugh, Buckshot Roberts and, most dangerous of all, bucktoothed little William Bonney — Billy the Kid. So, in no time at all, the landscape of Lincoln County was stained with blood.

Cal McDade could be heading for more than nester trouble. He wanted to hold his land — or land he claimed was his — and was prepared to fight for it. But his method of fighting could blow back in his face. Hard old buzzard though he was, he could wind up the prisoner or victim of the men around him. After all, both Murphy and McSween were dead by the time the hired gunslingers in their feud blasted the Lincoln County War to its end.

"Seems to me I need somebody with some regard for the Walking C," said McDade, finding his voice again.

"I believe I just heard you say your foreman, Ed Terry, was a man to be trusted," observed Herrick.

"Sure. And he is. He's a man with a solid business head, one whose commonsense you trust at once."

And a man who holed up behind a rock to bushwhack an unsuspecting victim as he rode by, Herrick commented in his mind. *He and that feller who was with him have a lot to answer for.* By now, Herrick had formed a shrewd idea as to the identity of the man who accompanied he of the broken matches, lying in the silica sand behind the rocks with a ready Winchester.

"What I mean is I need someone with a deeper understandin' of the Walking C, Dan. Someone like you," continued McDade. "After all, the outfit must mean plenty to you when you consider that you an' Elizabeth came close to marryin'. It ain't just that you built up a fast gun reputation as a peace officer up north but, damn it, you were almost married into the Walkin' C — almost my son-in-law . . . " He suddenly stopped talking again. Perhaps he was realising his own gall in bringing his daughter's name into it.

To Herrick, it was gall indeed. McDade, who once told him he was not good enough for Elizabeth, was almost begging him to take a hand in his war, to ramrod the unpredictable riff-raff bunking on his spread for gun-wages. And he was using sentiment as a lever.

Herrick's mouth quirked into a humourless smile. "You have a hell of a nerve, Cal," he drawled. In the old days, he would have addressed the old man as 'Major', just as everyone else did. As an Arizona pioneer and a cowman with plenty of savvy, he deserved his measure of respect. But now he had devalued himself. His wheedling approach and his appeal to Herrick's love for his dead daughter caused him to dwindle in Herrick's eyes. Even so, Herrick was almost sorry for him. Despite the gang he had gathered around him to fight off the ogre of the homesteader threat, he was scared and, at rock bottom, he knew he stood alone.

McDade raised a quivering hand as if to ward off verbal abuse. "I know what you're thinkin', Dan," he said hastily. "I don't blame you for bein' sore after the way I treated you when you said you wanted to marry my lovely girl. I was a damn fool back then. I acted too hastily and I've given it a lot of thought over the years. Fact is, I always wanted to make amends for it — came around to seein' I should make it up to you."

Herrick shrugged. "Sure, with a price tag attached, Cal — you want me to get in on your fight, not that it matters now, anyway, because nothin' will bring Elizabeth back. And do you figure Elizabeth would condone bushwhackin' an' the destruction of farms where poor folks are tryin' to make a livin'? Hell, you're insultin' her memory."

"I had no hand in any bushwhackin'," declared McDade. The wheedling attitude fell away, the lines of bitterness in his face deepened and his eyes glittered with the fanatical light again. "My men ran some blasted sodbusters off my land, sure, but I'll have no murder. Why not run sodbusters off? They're all damn Yanks, or kin to damn Yanks. Have you forgotten what Sheridan and his murderin' bluebellies did in the Shenandoah Valley; burnin' farms, killin' civilians? Have you forgotten Sherman's crimes in Georgia; murder, plunder and the burnin' of the city of Atlanta to a cinder? By God, I stood against Sherman's horde with General Hood's Texans — I *saw* what was done in Georgia! Sure, I'll run nesters off, but I'll give' em a chance to live an' start again. I'll have no murder — and that's the plain truth."

There was sincerity in his voice. It sounded like the honest and forthright Cal McDade of old. Herrick remembered the snapped matchstick lying in the hearth. Maybe the trusted foreman, Ed Terry and the man who sided him in the bushwhacking on the trail were playing their own game, unknown to McDade.

"I heard there was a murder, Cal — a man named Rogerson, shot outside his cabin," he said levelly. He carefully omitted reference to the more recent killing of the rider whose body he had placed beneath the cairn.

"I know there's talk that Walkin' C was involved," growled McDade. "That ain't so. I heard Rogerson had a loose mouth and said too much in a saloon. You know what that could lead to in this country at the best of times, Dan. The only reason they mention my outfit is because we're the only ones who've made our feelin's about nesters well known. The other ranchmen on this range, Dick Schultz, of the DS, and Charlie Costain, of the Box-Bar, are acceptin' 'em, bucklin' under to the blasted Washington gang and their Homestead Act."

Maybe, thought Herrick, just maybe, the old buzzard truly had no part in the killings. The sign was that he was being hoodwinked by the smooth and plausible Ed Terry, in whose savvy he placed such trust. And Terry was certainly a bushwhacker.

Some deep conspiracy could be in progress at the Walking C but maybe this new, half-cracked Cal McDade was so blinded by his anti-sodbuster fury and so trapped by his personal fantasy of fighting the war the South lost that he had no inkling of what was going on under his nose.

McDade suddenly changed his tone, becoming more confidential and almost fatherly.

"Look, Dan, what I wanted to say to you when I got you alone is that I really do want to make it up to you," he began. "I shouldn't have treated you the way I did. There's somethin' I want to put to you . . . " He broke off abruptly as a pounding of impatient hoofs sounded from the yard. Then there was a hubbub of indistinct yells and a thumping of boots and ringing of spurs as men ran up the steps and across the boards of the gallery.

The rancher turned to the door and stiffened as a torrent of bodies surged into the room, men with dangerous, wild-eyed faces — and naked sixguns. In the lead was one of the two riders whom Herrick had encountered as he neared the Walking C headquarters. His Colt was levelled at Herrick and his free hand was flung forward, pointing at him accusingly.

"Major!" he bellowed. "He killed Floyd an' old Dad Samuelson! We found their bodies in the brush!"

5

CAL McDADE jerked his angry face back towards Herrick as still more crowded into the room.

"By God! Killin' my hands on my graze!" he roared. "This is part of your backin' up damned sodbusters. An' you a Texas man an' a free-range cattleman — I can't believe it!"

Herrick cursed himself for a damned fool. He should have known that the double blast of his .45 and the report of the Winchester would cause the two riders to investigate. They had not really swallowed the yarn about killing a rattler. Maybe, too, a first circling of buzzards had alerted them to the position of the corpses. They had allowed him to ride deeper into Walking C territory and he was now truly bottled up. He faced drawn guns

88

and itchy trigger fingers, caught in a room rapidly filling with hostile men. He was a damned fool.

If shooting started now, he could only lose out. He might take some Walking C men with him but, in the end, he would be gunned down, as easy a target as a fish in a barrel.

He remembered the window immediately behind him, the big window, divided into panes by wooden frames. The whole structure came down almost to the floor. Cal McDade built this house years before and the desert air coupled with season upon season of blazing sunshine would have dried out the wooden interstices to a crispy brittleness. A desperate idea formed in Herrick's mind as he backed away in the direction of the window.

Glowering faces and wildly flourished sixguns bore close upon him.

"Don't start shootin' here, you blasted half-wits!" shouted McDade.

Herrick suddenly began a blind, stumbling, backward run as speedily as he could. Trusting that the wood in the window was old and dry enough to yield, he hurled himself at it backwards. He ducked his head low and held his hands close against his chest as his spine smote the window. He met the resistance of wood and glass — then felt it give.

He pitched out of the room with a rending and crashing. A jagged edge of glass slashed at a shirtsleeve and another jabbed through the tough material of his pants and into his thigh.

With an impact which gusted breath from his lungs, he landed on his back in the dust of the yard beside the house as splintered wood and shattered glass fell around him. Fighting for breath and staggering to his feet, he snatched out his gun then fired a couple of slugs into the dry adobe beside the window. A stream of profanities issued from beyond the aparture, but the slugs deterred the bunch inside the house from charging it and firing at him. They would not risk framing themselves in the window with a skilled gunhand only yards beyond it.

Herrick began to run alongside the house, making for the expanse of the yard immediately fronting it where his bronc was hitched and, as he set off, he heard McDade's voice bellowing: "Don't shoot, damn you! I don't want him dead!"

Trying to find the wind and energy to run as fast as he could, he also attempted to think on two different levels. He was aware of stinging lacerations caused by the glass and he hoped he was not badly cut and was losing blood. He was also aware that, probably, the Walking C men were heading for the gallery, anticipating that he would make for the bronc.

That proved to be the case. Just as he emerged from the side of the house, the gunhands tumbled out of its front door and on to the gallery. Gun in hand, he hared across the dusty apron of the yard towards the trough, the hitch-rack and the bronc, centred in the yard and full in front of the gallery. The blue of gun metal showed among the men of the gallery and a sixgun exploded.

Herrick heard Cal McDade yelling that curious caution again, this time, nearly shrieking: *"No! Don't shoot him!"*

Driving his legs like pistons, Herrick reached the trough just as another gun blasted. As he was in the act of diving behind the cover of the stone trough, he felt the hot bee-sting of the bullet as it grazed his right shoulder. He sprawled in the dust behind the trough, jamming his .45 back into its holster and gritting his teeth against the nag of pain starting in the shoulder.

Now, he had to concentrate on loosing the bronc from the rack, getting into the saddle and splitting the wind out of the ranch yard. On the ranch house gallery, some of the Walking C men were showing caution by lying flat on the boards. Herrick was no longer a running target, crossing a wide-open space. He was settled behind good cover and in an advantageous position for so good a gunslinger.

He rolled on his back, growling to himself because of the bullet graze to his shoulder and the cuts elsewhere about his body. Quickly, he hauled out his Colt again and thumbed slugs from his shell-belt into the vacant chambers.

"Damn!" he breathed as he felt his gunhand already stiffening as the result of the graze. His shoulder seemed not to have been drilled through, nor was the bone shattered. Hopefully, he was merely experiencing the shock of a severe graze. In a hole like this, the last thing he needed was an impaired gun hand.

For the moment, the actions quietened, with the men on the gallery obviously waiting for his next move. Squinting up at the nearby hitch-rack, where his horse shifted uneasily because of the shooting, he gathered his breath then rolled over, came to his knees and kept his head well down behind the trough, knowing he was invisible to the men at the house.

Deliberately, he holstered his sixgun again then sprang upwards, grabbing at the bronc's leathers, hitched to the rail. He yanked it loose and was forking the saddle as the men across the yard came to life and another gun blasted. Herrick ducked as a slug screamed over his head, rowelled the animal hard and yipped a throaty urging. The bronc lurched forward and Herrick swung his body over, offside from the house and rode low, flattened out, Indian fashion, along the neck of the horse.

The bronc lunged off across the yard as guns roared again and bullets swarmed past its switching tail. Herrick was hanging on almost by his eyebrows, steering the bronc for the big, arched gateway. The bullet-bite nagged more insistently at the flesh of his shoulder and he thought that the Walking C gunnies would soon be mounted on better horseflesh than his own and in full pursuit. The bronc had put in much hard travelling and was now in need of feed. It was in no shape for a long chase.

Mount and rider passed through the gate and, almost at once, Herrick departed from the hardened earth of the ranch-trail and pressed the bronc over the scrubby, desert-edge rangeland, searching his memory for the geography of these parts as he went.

The drumming of hoofs sounded behind him and grew louder.

"C'mon, hoss, give all you have," he hissed. The little horse lunged onward gamely, raising a banner of dust with its hoofs. Herrick glanced back and, through the dust, saw the bobbing blobs that were Walking C riders, coming hard on his heels. The outfit always kept a good *remuda* of cow-ponies and, from what he had seen of the animals wearing McDade's brand, he knew this was one department in which its standards had not declined. Keeping ahead of the pursuers on his jaded bronc would be no small order.

The injury in his shoulder burned and the cuts from the window glass stung his flesh. Already, he was beginning to feel used-up. He tried to spur more speed out of the bronc, feeling he should apologise to it for inflicting such punishment and trying to push it beyond its limit. In his backtrail, the pursuing horsemen drummed louder. Any second now, they would be close enough to sling shots at him.

He travelled up a rise of land, rode over its crest and, on the downward slope, found a bunch of Cal McDade's longhorns grazing full across his path. There were perhaps a hundred head and Herrick saw some salvation in their presence.

The dun and black cattle, with their seven-foot spans of horn, stirred uneasily at the rapid approach of the mounted man and he angled his animal off towards the edge of the herd. He whipped off his hat and, constantly wincing against the pain in his shoulder, waved it vigorously and set up a harsh hoorawing.

"Eee-yah! Eee-yah! Git back, dogies! Git back! Git back!" he bellowed, like a demented drag rider shoving a sluggish herd uptrail.

The animals nearest to him pranced back in alarm, then turned about and began to run towards the centre of the bobbing mass of horns. The other cattle caught the panicky infection, about-tailed and began to run up the slope. They gathered momentum, becoming a horned river.

"Hoo-yaw! Git along! Git along!" roared Herrick, giving chase. The beef-on-hoof drummed yet faster up the rise.

The Walking C riders came over the crest, full into the face of a shifting mass of thundering longhorns, coming in a near-stampede. Herrick grinned sardonically as, just before the sight of the pursuing riders was blotted out by the fog of dust stirred by the beeves, he

97

saw them breaking up and scattering.

He turned the bronc and resumed his flight dead ahead, knowing he could only have hindered the riders temporarily. Trying to fathom exactly where he was on the Walking C range, he saw a stand of live-oaks and remembered.

He was close to the locality known as the Breaks. It was a tangled region of dried-up watercourses and towering boulders, tumbled country in which a man might lose pursuers — if he had a good enough start and a sturdy mount. A natural boundary of the legally held Walking C range, the Breaks was an inhospitable tract of up-ended terrain, harsh and arid and fit only for snakes and scorpions. Cattle instinctively kept away from it but, occasionally, a steer blundered into its baffling tangles and, if its bawling did not early attract some nearby Walking C wrangler, its bones might be found months or even years afterwards. No ranch hand went into the place willingly, which was why Herrick now made a dead-run towards it, making use of the time he had gained by hazing the herd back towards the pursuing riders.

He knew, however, that it would not take long for the riders, on their superior mounts, to remuster and quickly pick up his trail. The ground under the bronc's hoofs became more broken, more streaked with tracts of silica sand and less supportive of reasonable graze. Soon, he was surrounded by sun-blasted boulders, some higher than horse and rider, saluting saguaro cactus, Joshua trees and catclaw, the tough and enduring vegetation which had clung to Arizona's desert face for unknown lengths of time.

Suddenly, he was riding down a slope, into an arroyo, a long dried water-gully, where fantastically shaped rocks were arrayed along the sloping sides like frozen monsters. Now, he was getting into the Breaks proper. Here, he must give the bronc a chance to find its own way and not risk a slip or tumble which could cause a broken leg.

"Easy, now, Hoss," he soothed. "We ain't leavin' any trail in this place — not one anybody but an Apache could follow, anyway. Just you take an easy walk. You've sure worked hard, little partner."

The bronc, seeming to understand him, walked at a slow pace along the arroyo bed. It was lathered and steaming and, after a brief spell, Herrick came down from the saddle with difficulty and walked beside it, holding the reins, by way of easing the animal's burden.

He found he was walking with difficulty, with every bone in his body aching. Cuts and lacerations about his limbs stung him persistently, the bullet wound in his shoulder ground at him agonisingly and, for the first time, he saw that a large patch of blood was half-dry on his shirt. Anxiously, he glanced back at the sand and rocks he and the bronc had just traversed.

He seemed not to be dripping a clear trail of blood which the Walking C pursuers could follow.

He kept on, traipsing deeper into the Breaks with the late afternoon sun beating hard on the bronc and himself. His mouth was like the inside of a furnace and his tongue and lips felt like the dried leather of old boots. He hoped he might chance upon water in one of the many arroyos which criss-crossed the Breaks like gigantic axe-gouges, but knew it was a forlorn hope. Now and then, a red haze began to swim before his vision and he shook his head, trying to drive it away.

"Sure is hot, Hoss," he told the bronc. "Hotter than anythin' I remember. Anythin' I *can* ever remember. You ever know anythin' as hot as this in all your born days?" His voice croaked and he knew he was babbling like a drunk. It was the old desert man's reaction of simply talking to his horse for companionship in the face of the fear of wilderness, sun and thirst. He plodded on, leading the horse, now and then staggering, talking all the time and frequently telling himself aloud to keep his voice down in case Cal McDade's riders were somewhere behind him.

He plodded on along the arroyo bed, through a maze of high rocks and cactus, fighting off bouts of lightheadedness, conscious that he was on the edge of delirium and not knowing where he was bound. For all he knew, he might blunder back the way he came and meet up with the pursuers. In moments of mental clarity, he wondered about the behaviour of Cal McDade. At one moment, the rancher was furious about the killing of two of his hired ruffians then, when the rest of the gunnies showed equal vengeful resentment, he was roaring for Herrick not to be shot.

"That old buzzard sure takes some fathoming," he croaked to the bronc as the pair stumbled on through the snarled-up gully. "Some day, we'll understand what goes on around here,

Hoss — if we live long enough."

They came to a ragged escarpment, a wall of rock, running along one side of the arroyo. In it, half-hidden by tumbled boulders and big clumps of hardy yucca, was what amounted to a cave, a coolly inviting opening which offered shade and rest. Herrick yanked the bronc's leathers, steering the animal's head towards it and trudged up the shaley slope which was its doorstep.

"Might find water in there," he said, though he knew there was no real hope. "Damned if I ain't growin' old after all. I should have filled the canteen at the Santa Clara Sink when I had the chance. Just didn't figure you an' me would be in for any dry journeys to-day!"

Nests of rattlers or sidewinders were more likely to be found in such a cave than water, but there was a chance of rest, shade from the beating sun and an opportunity to gather his half-mad thoughts into some kind of order inside its dark mouth. There was room enough for both man and animal under the ragged portal and Herrick led the horse in gratefully.

There was no water and, mercifully, no sign of snakes; just a cluster of big spiders and a half-asleep gila monster which wakened as the bronc clattered in then made its lizard way out into the sunshine. The cave was a mere fissure, going back into the rock for a few yards and ending in a blank wall. It smelt of centuries of arid darkness, but it was cool after the merciless hammering of the sun.

The bronc snorted with satisfaction as it encountered the shade and Herrick sat down on the rocky floor, just inside the cave's entrance, resting his back against its craggy wall. His feet burned and ached and his whole body felt as if it had been dragged behind a wild horse. His head swam and the haze which now and again obscured his vision returned with greater frequency. The blood-patch on his shirt was bigger than he first thought. Groggily, he looked out and upward at the sun, trying to fix some idea of his position and in which direction he had been travelling. He was incapable of making any judgement.

"Doggone, it's like bein' drunk, Hoss — except there's no fun in it," he rasped to the bronc.

Suddenly, he was aware of the dim clop of horses and the jingle of ringbits. He listened intently, thinking maybe the sounds came out of his fevered fancy.

No, there was certainly a genuine sound of horses on the still, dry air — and growing louder. Riders, possibly a couple of them, were approaching at a slow, steady walk. Herrick squinted cautiously out of the cave and saw that the arroyo was empty. Yet the horses clopped on, seeming to draw nearer.

Herrick frowned and listened. Then he realised that the sound came from immediately above him. It dawned on him that the escarpment in which the cave opened, carried some kind of rough trail along its top. The riders — he was fairly sure there were two of them — were travelling along it and must be just about above his head. The cautious clatter of hoofs grew yet louder then stopped.

A voice which Herrick had heard only recently, floated down into the arroyo. "Dammit, Lafe, there's no use in goin' further an' I sure ain't aimin' to lose myself in that maze," it said. "I'm stoppin' for a smoke."

"Might just as well. He's given us the slip, thanks to gaining time by hazing that beef back towards us," said a second voice. It had silky delivery and precise diction. It, too, was a voice Herrick had heard before. "Still, I'd like to see this Herrick put out of the way. He's nosy and interfering and seems like he has brains enough to be an obstacle to our plans."

The other chuckled drily. "Well, we have our own way of settlin' the hash of jaspers who look like puttin' a hitch in what we aim to do, huh, Lafe? First Rogerson, then Holbrook. An' it was easy as pie."

"Yes, and I'll settle Herrick in due time. If he hangs around this country, it'll be him or me in the way we understand best. I knew that the minute I saw him in Centro. We're the same breed, him and me. Meantime, we should think about moving towards getting our hands on the spread and putting paid to that half-mad old McDade."

There was a brief silence, then something floated down past the mouth of the cave and landed on the rocks only inches from where Herrick sat. It had been tossed over the ledge on which the riders had halted right over Herrick's head. It was a spent match, snapped in the middle to make a 'V'.

Herrick pictured the pair, sitting on halted horses just above his head and hoped he could hang on to a clear memory of what he had heard and retain it under the threat of encroaching giddiness and delirium. The two riders, obviously separated from their Walking C henchmen and holding a highly confidential exchange in this isolated place, were the Walking C foreman, Ed Terry and the fancy, long-haired gunfighter whose name he now knew to be Lafe.

They were the pair who had bushwhacked the unknown sodbuster he found on the trail. Almost certainly, they had killed Rogerson also.

And they were plotting to get rid of Cal McDade and grab his Walking C spread.

6

HERRICK sat motionless in the entrance to the cave, straining to catch every word floating down into the drywash.

"You figure the others might have found him?" asked Terry.

"No. He gave himself a good chance of gaining ground when he worked that stunt with the cattle. Those with McDade might be making some effort to find him, but most are half-hearted. They might be sore about Floyd and old Samuelson but I'll bet they're doing what you and I are doing, — hanging around the fringe of this God-awful place and smoking. You know everyone is pretty well sick of old McDade's fool antics and crazy obsessions." The gunfighter's well educated voice dripped scorn.

"Figure any of 'em will give us

trouble when we make our move?" Ed Terry enquired.

Lafe, the gunfighter, laughed harshly. "No. Most will get the hell out. They're scared of me and they'll jump when I shout. They're penny-ante scum looking for easy pay. We'll soon get real forty-and-found, sore rump wranglers in these hard times. The essential thing is that we have McDade's signature on the papers Cory is drawing up and bringing from Tucson. Once we get McDade out of the way and put your ranch savvy and my money savvy to work, we'll be high style ranchers. Then, no more scraping around the poverty stricken edges of life for us."

"Sure," retorted Ed Terry. "It can't come soon enough. I'm sick of hirin' out to other men."

The butt of a Bull Durham cigarette dropped down past the mouth of the fissure and landed close to the tell-tale match.

Terry's voice came again: "Well, I guess we should just go back an' meet up with the others an' tell 'em we had no luck."

The clop of horses sounded again and Herrick pictured the pair turning their mounts around on the narrow ledge trail above his head. Then the hoofs began a steady tramping, gradually fading away.

Herrick remained still, telling himself that, even if he blacked out, he must remember what he had heard. Again, he hoped delirium was not swamping his consciousness and that he really had heard the ranch foreman and Lafe, the professional gunslinger, in conversation and the whole experience was not simply a kind of audible mirage.

With the arroyo silent again, he stirred. The act of rising from his sitting position caused aches in his bones and his punished body nagged at him even more fiercely. He grabbed hold of the saddle and hung on to the bronc for a couple of minutes to gather his strength.

"I don't know where we're goin',

Hoss, but we have to get our butts out of this hell-hole," he told the animal. He still would not risk riding the treacherous terrain of the drywash bottoms and he cautiously led the bronc out to resume his stumbling march.

His shirt was soaked in sweat, his vision was now almost permanently blurred but, with the sun now westering, he knew that if he kept it to his right, he was heading north. And northward lay Centro. Herrick aimed for the town, lured by the hope of water, food and rest.

He mumbled to the bronc constantly, in an attempt to hang on to his sanity.

"What do you make of this Lafe feller, Hoss?" he asked. "Can't recollect any gunslinger of that name an' I heard the monikers most of 'em go by. Sure talks fancy, though. Sounds like he came from a long way east in the first place.

"An' how about this mess McDade

is in? The trouble is the old fool can't know what's cookin' under his nose because he's still in the thick of the big war an' he's got it all mixed up with his war on the homesteaders. Talked about having something to put to me. I figure he . . . he . . . "

Stumbling on uneven rocks, he lost his vision for an instant and came close to blacking out. The wound in his shoulder flamed with pain and the cuts from the glass stung more agonisingly. He clutched at the bronc's saddle-rig for support, hung on to it and staggered onward, using the animal for support.

" . . . I figure he wanted me to sling my gun into his damnfool fight against the nesters, Hoss. Well, by God, he should know better. I'm havin' no part of runnin' plain, simple folk off the land. If that girl, Dorcas, an' her brother are . . . are . . . " He staggered and stumbled and his voice became a thirst-cracked growl. " . . . if they're standin' up to McDade and his rannihans,

I'm with 'em, by cracky ... still ... still, I kind of believe him when he says he knows nothin' about the bushwhackin' affairs." He gave a sudden, cracked laugh. "After all, *we* know who backshot the nester we found on the trail, don't we, Hoss? Yes, sir, a feller who snaps his matches after he lights a smoke an' another who wears a belt buckle with a big longhorn head on it. Because that's what we found in the sand behind that rock, where they lay waitin': not only broken matches, but the plain print of a longhorn where that long-haired Lafe lay on his belly ... "

He spluttered and croaked, cursed his aching body and the choking thirst and progressed drunkenly beside the faithful animal. " ... yes, Hoss, we have to hang on an' keep alive. We have things to do, business to finish. Got to do somethin' for McDade ... got to ... maybe he *is* half crazy but he can't know that the snakes he's gathered around him aim to steal the

Walkin' C from him but, by God, he's Elizabeth's old man an' we have to do somethin' for her sake . . . Elizabeth, now there was a girl, Hoss, too bad you never knew her . . . she was a girl in a million . . . "

His speech became garbled and most of the progress was now being made by the animal, with Herrick hanging on to the saddle-rig, simply being dragged along. He blundered on like a sailor on an uncharted sea. The sun sank deeper and the spiny landscape became blood-red.

Somewhere, in the setting of a crazy dream, they rounded a stand of organpipe cactus, staggered through gnarled rocks and came to a tract of shaley land which gave way to tawny grass slopes, leading down to a small stream. Herrick had a blurred vision of a squat homestead building and a barn in the distance, beyond the ribbon of the stream.

Then a figure was approaching him and he was convinced he was dead.

115

For it was a girl. *Elizabeth!*

"We didn't make it, Hoss," he croaked. "But we must have done some good somewhere in our no-account lives, for the Lord has been merciful to us. We're going over the Jordan, an' here comes Elizabeth to meet us!"

The girl's face swam into his fogged vision and he could not understand why Elizabeth's dark hair had become golden. Then he reasoned that it was probably her halo for, if they gave out halos in heaven, Elizabeth surely rated one. Her face swam nearer and he felt her hands grip him, one on each shoulder.

Then blackness overwhelmed him.

* * *

She was not Elizabeth.

She was Dorcas, the homesteader girl. Herrick recognised her now as he struggled up from suffocating depths. Consciousness broke over him and he

116

supposed he had fainted.

He found he was in a bed in a lamplit room and he presumed that night lay beyond the curtained window in the far corner. Dorcas was bent over him, considering him with deep concern. There was another face behind hers, one he remembered from the old days in Centro, wrinkled, with a droopy moustache and shrewd eyes behind steel-rimmed glasses. Cynical old Doc Grogan.

"How d'you feel?" asked the doctor.

"Stiff an' sore all over," muttered Herrick.

"You're likely to be," said the medico. "The last time I saw cuts like you have on your arms and legs they were on a fellow who made a hasty exit through the window of a lady's bedroom while it was closed. I believe he was assisted by the boot of a husband who had returned unexpectedly." The doctor ended on a self-conscious cough and looked towards Dorcas as if his conversation was tending toward the inappropriate. Then, on a weightier note, added: "Miss Holbrook has suffered a severe blow, I fear."

Herrick considered the girl. Now that his vision was clearer, he could see that she had recently been crying.

"The Walking C crew have killed my brother, Bob," she said with a sob in her voice. "He was found on the trail — shot in the back."

The memory of the homesteader lying dead in the dust smote Herrick like a hammer blow. He sat up suddenly then gasped as pain knifed at his shoulder. He sank back against the pillow, gritting his teeth.

"Take it easy, son," advised Doc Grogan. "That's a severe slice from a slug you have there. I cleaned and bandaged it. It isn't infected, but it will be sore for some time. I cleaned the remainder of your cuts with iodine."

"Your brother? Bushwhacked?" exclaimed Herrick.

"That's exactly the word," put in Doc Grogan. "Bob was found by the

Candlins, three homesteader brothers he'd just visited. He'd been backshot with a Winchester. Curiously, somebody had covered his body with a heap of rocks."

Herrick slowly eased himself up on his good elbow. "I know somethin' about it," he said with a guilty glance at Dorcas. "I found him in the first place. I covered him with the rocks so the body could remain preserved for identification. I had the notion that I'd be able to tell whatever law was in Centro about the body. Then I found old Yawberry was still around and guessed there was still no real county organisation and no sheriff. After that, things happened fast and I got into a bad hole out at the Walkin' C. Still, I should have acted on findin' the body — done somethin' definite about informin' the authorities."

"You knew all the time?" Dorcas gasped. "All the time you were talking to me in Centro, you knew about Bob lying on the trail out yonder, dead?"

"Sorry, Miss Holbrook, but I didn't know he was your brother. If you'll forgive me, I figure your brother would be a much younger man," Herrick said penitently. "I never connected the man I found with you."

"Bob was my half-brother," she said. "My mother married a man much older than herself, a widower with a son, Bob. I came along late, which is why Bob was so much older. He was closer than many real brothers and very protective. No woman could ask for a better brother. And no community could ask for a better member. That was why he was murdered: because he wanted decent behaviour and a decent place to live."

"Sure," rumbled the doctor. "But you can be sure Bob didn't die in vain. A lot of people will be stirred by his death. We did nothing for too long and remained complacent, or maybe just too scared, even when young Rogerson was killed. I figure that, with Bob, it will be different."

Herrick noted the steely glint in the medical man's eye. There was a jut to his jaw which suggested he was only just keeping the lid on his anger. He had always liked Doc Grogan who, like many a frontier medico, was a bit of a mystery. Some said he had been a Civil War surgeon who had gone to ground in a place like Centro for his own reasons. Nobody asked whether he wore blue pants or grey in the big war and he never spoke about it. He did his best for all who needed his services. Sometimes his bills were paid but, often, they were not. Doc took it all philosophically and he had a knack of turning up where he was required, as seemed to be the case now.

He looked at Herrick and there was a knitting of unspoken rapport when their eyes met.

"I remember you when you worked for McDade," said Doc. "I recall you bringing a puncher with a broken leg into my office one time."

"That was Karl Lundgren, the best

121

wrangler on the spread at breakin' a bronc — but he fell off a corral rail when he was takin' a smoke. Karl laughed loudest of all afterward. We had some happy times on the Walkin' C back in those days." Herrick shook his head wistfully, chiefly remembering that, back in those days, Elizabeth was there to make the place happy.

"But they're not so happy now, huh?" The doctor's eyes considered him keenly then he added: "I heard you rode out to McDade's place."

"Sure, but not because I aimed to throw my gun in on his side, Doc. I came back with certain notions about McDade an' his crew."

"I guess you just naturally would if the cuts I doctored indicate the kind of welcome they gave you."

Dorcas handed Herrick a cup of water, poured from a large pitcher. "Drink this. You must be parched," she said.

Herrick took the cup and, almost instinctively, reached out with his free hand to touch the girl's hand. "I'm sorry about Bob. A lot of things have to be put right around here an' I intend to do what I can to put 'em right."

Dorcas bit her lip then said slowly: "Not through violence. Too much has been done violently — Bob and Rogerson killed and all those simple homestead folk scared away. We need peaceful means to getting a peaceful land."

"Dorcas, you know what I reckon this gent needs most of all after a spell of rest? I'd say he'd relish some solid grub. It's likely to do more good than the attentions of an old country sawbones like me," put in Doc.

The girl's grief-clouded face was brightened by a slight smile. "I guess you're right. I suppose I was so intent on getting him some help when I spotted him across the creek where The Breaks peter out on to our claim that I never considered feeding him. I'll fix something." She turned and left the small bedroom.

"She's a good girl and ought not to be put through this kind of misery," grunted Doc. "Seems she got you across the creek when you were all-in. She bedded you down here, cleaned up some of your wounds, stabled your horse, watered and fed him then rode the buckboard into town to get me. She arrived right after the Candlin brothers had brought Bob's body in and I'd just finished examining the corpse. She bore up pretty darned well when I broke the news to her."

"She has courage, Doc. I saw some of it myself. She was handin' out fistfuls of hot hell to some homesteaders who were fixin' to quit," commented Herrick.

"But this could cause her to break. She said to me she might pull up stakes and return to teaching school in the East," said Doc. "Her kind of courage needs the support of good men. I knew Yawberry was drunk, saw him staggering down the street with a bottle in his hand earlier. There was no point in expecting him to do anything about a backshooting outside town limits. So I made a few notes about the condition of Bob's body. Later, I make a fuller report which I'll put into the hands of the US Marshal in Tucson later. For the time being, we must concentrate on Dorcas' immediate need to see her brother buried decently. I took Bob up the street to Hasselhoff's funeral parlour on my own buckboard. Then we made a brief call at Preacher Weems' shack and arranged for him to read a burial service tomorrow. Finally, Dorcas and I came back here and found you still totally exhausted."

"Doggone, Doc. It's a good thing Centro has you as a resident."

"Just a case of trying to do the right thing by a girl like Dorcas when she's all but overwhelmed by violence," shrugged the doctor.

"There could be more yet, in spite of her hopes," Herrick observed quietly. "I had to elevate a couple of McDade's rannihans. They tried to kill me.

Jumped me clean in the first place but I took care of 'em. It was self-defence, Doc, but there were no witnesses. With luck, I got away from the rest of his crew, but they might track me down here an' come lookin' for trouble. I'll fight 'em if I have to, but I can't risk any of 'em gettin' their hands on Dorcas. Maybe I should get out of here fast."

Doc gave his moustache a thoughtful tug. "Or maybe there's a case for sticking around — you, me and friends — and making sure we put an end to the Walking C's antics for good and all and making the place safe for Dorcas and those like her."

"An' friends, Doc? I figured we were pretty much alone in this."

"Oh, we have potential allies who need a little spurring into action. A kind of notion has been seeping into my brain in the last half hour or so."

The aroma of cooking drifted into the bedroom. Together with Doc's mysterious but heartening words, it made Herrick feel better. He eased himself up in the bed yet further.

"Sounds like you're thinkin' of some kind of action, Doc."

"Well, it could come to pass once I get all my thoughts into shape. We could yet start to put things right."

"It's a tall order, but I'm willin' to get down to cases with you an' settle scores. By the way, any idea who the long-haired gunnie known as Lafe really is?"

"Sure, calls himself Lafe Pendexter, someone McDade brought in to give weight to his insane war on the homesteaders. I heard it whispered he's really Larry Pringle."

Herrick gave a long, low whistle. "Larry Pringle — so that's who! I knew his name would mean something when I heard it. Larry Pringle, from Indian Territory and the Texas Panhandle! I never met up with him but I know Judge Parker over at Fort Smith, Arkansas, is plumb eager to have him on his famous gallows an' in the hands of his big German hangman, George

Maledon. Heard it said Pringle came off a wealthy New England family an' once had a respectable post in business with his father. Then somethin' went wrong, he drifted out to the frontier an' made a gunslinger of himself. Somehow, he's survived after most of his kind have bit the dust."

"That's substantially the background on Pringle I heard myself," said Doc. "There's a string of killings behind him and he's dodging warrants. That's why he's keeping well away from Texas and Indian Territory."

"Seems he's tired of gunslingin'," observed Herrick. "He knows what most of us know, except McDade an' some old-timers like him: that the days of the wild guns are disappearin' fast. He wants to settle down with a whole skin."

"What makes you say that?"

"I can tell you, Doc, that McDade's foreman, Ed Terry, an' our long-haired friend bushwhacked Bob Holbrook an' I know from their own lips that they killed Rogerson, too. The pattern is clear. They want to destroy anyone capable of intelligent opposition because they aim to steal the Walkin' C. Then they'll call the tune on these ranges and clear out the remainin', leaderless homesteaders when it suits 'em. One knows the money markets an' the other the Western cattle game, so they figure they can run the spread far better than an old Texas, trail-drivin' pioneer like Cal McDade. I heard things in The Breaks an' I know somebody named Cory is in it with 'em."

Doc Grogan leaned forward eagerly. "That can only be Azell Cory. He's a lawyer from Tucson and a crooked one by all accounts," he said.

"Well, he's drawn up papers an' it's plain that they pass the Walking C title to those two jaspers. They don't give a damn for McDade's war against the homesteaders or for the rannihans he's gathered around him. Grabbin' his ranch is their real game. They'll probably find a convenient way of gettin' rid of him after he's been forced to sign away the title."

Quickly, Herrick outlined the evidence of the broken matches and the imprint of the longhorn buckle and told the doctor what he heard when holed up in The Breaks. Dorcas arrived with boiled beef, potatoes and buttered biscuits for both of them. She gave Herrick another smile, noting his eagerness to wire into the food. It was as if keeping busy helped to ease her grief.

"I'll fix coffee," she said, leaving again.

Herrick continued his tale as both ate. Doc Grogan heard it out with grunts and nods between mouthfuls.

"Well, I can tell you what I know about Azell Cory," he said at length. "I have a doctor friend over in Tucson and I go up there once in a while to read up on the medical journals he gets from the East. Most doctors and lawyers get to know the professional rumours going around, specially in a small town. He told me there was an unsavoury scandal around a will left by a patient of his. Cory was the lawyer involved and, though it was all so cleverly done that no one could prove anything in law, a heap of money got into the wrong hands and no small amount went to Cory. If you heard Cory's name mentioned, you can bet those two are backing their play with right smart legal trickery."

The medico paused as Dorcas brought in coffee. Again, she smiled at Herrick as she placed the cup on the small bedside table then straightened the pillow behind his back so he could relax more easily. "I'm so glad you were not too badly hurt," she murmured. "Doctor Grogan says you'll be fine after a rest. And your little horse seems to be well enough now that he's been watered and fed."

"I guess we're both as hard-wearing as each other," grinned Herrick. "Though it's likely the bronc has the most brains."

Dorcas smiled her sad smile again and he was aware of her sheer, womanly goodness which was like balm in a world of hard knocks and violence.

The girl took out the men's empty plates, obviously intent on keeping herself busy.

Doc Grogan pulled at his moustache thoughtfully. "Now that you tell me there's something afoot at Walking C, with Azell Cory involved, it seems to me there could be a case for mounting a showdown and clearing up the whole business before it goes from bad to worse," he stated darkly.

Herrick started. "Sounds like vigilante talk, Doc. That don't seem fittin' in Doc Grogan, the upstandin' citizen who goes around doin' good."

"Well, maybe old Doc Grogan wasn't always a battered old country doctor," rumbled Doc. "Some might say he became one because he was offering the Lord the devil's leavings. Still, maybe there comes a time when a few half-forgotten skills have to be called on for the common good."

The doctor purposely caused one side of his frock-coat to fall open and Herrick saw a big Peacemaker Colt nestling in a holster against his vest.

"What exactly are you drivin' at, Doc?"

"Oh, just a little something in the way of civic duty. You know, nobody will remember Chester A Arthur among the great presidents of the United States. It's almost a joke to mention him in the same breath as Washington and Lincoln. Still, he had a strong point when he called for the exercise of better citizenship in Arizona Territory right after all the hoorawin' around Tombstone. Could be we have to exercise some citizenship to make sure Pringle and Terry don't oust McDade and take over these ranges. McDade might be bad enough, but at least he's the devil we know. With the right will and methods, we can settle him in good time. Bad as he is, the old fool does have legal title to his lands. We can't see him robbed."

"What're you cookin', Doc?"

"All in good time, son. Look, I'm going to slip away for a spell, but I'll come back before morning. Our first priority is to see Bob properly buried. You rest here, keeping that Colt handy against any sudden arrival of Walking C men and make sure Dorcas is safe. I'll persuade the poor girl to get some rest. After to-morrow, maybe we should think in terms of a last battle to finish a war."

"Doggone, Doc, there's more to you than shows on your hide."

Behind the spectacles, the doctor's eyes twinkled. "You're a Westerner, son, you know that's true of many men you run into out here. Just bide here a spell. Work those fingers once in a while and massage your arm to get the stiffness out."

"To make sure I can handle a gun, Doc?"

"Well, it might just come to that,

but don't worry Dorcas with any talk of violence."

A short time later, as the sound of Dorcas washing the dishes issued from the small kitchen of the homestead shack, Herrick put a hand to the window curtain, just reachable from the bed. He drew it across and looked out on to the night scene. He could see clear across the creek to the up-ended country of The Breaks, beyond which lay the Walking C holdings.

There were magnificent banners of glowing crimson staining the sky over McDade's place, as if the sun was reluctant to die completely.

It was the typical blood-sky of the Arizona desert country, a sight to see yet, to Herrick in his present mood, sinister in its symbolism. He wondered what danger might come from that quarter, even to-night.

He reached across to his gun-gear, lying on a chair, took his shell-belt and holster. He checked the chambers of his .45, thumbed fresh cartridges into empty chambers. Quickly, in case Dorcas entered and found him handling the weapon, he shoved the sixgun under his pillow. Then he put the gear back on the chair and dropped his shirt over it so she would not notice the empty holster.

The movements made him realise how stiff his gun-arm was. Obeying the doctor, he began to rub it with his other hand.

From outside, came the clop of the buckboard borrowed from Dorcas going on whatever mysterious mission Doc had in hand.

7

PREACHER WEEMS had no degrees in theology and his battered, flat-crowned black hat was about his only gesture towards the formal dress of a clergyman. The remainder of his attire made him appear more a mule-skinner than a man of the cloth. Preacher and Padre Bonaventuro, the aged Franciscan friar who cared for the Mexicans, were the only spiritual guides Centro possessed.

He was a 'shoutin' Methodist' whose vocation was to proclaim the Gospel — or, rather, to holler it — at the inhabitants of this portion of the frontier, a few of whom were pious islands in a sea of the sin-hardened. Preacher was somewhere in middle age. He was small and thin but could roar with the ferocity of a stricken buffalo when the spirit moved him to preach.

He had his tender side, however, which showed when he met the victims of tragedy.

It showed now in his sympathetic expression as Preacher stood at the gate in the rickety fence surrounding Centro's cemetery, a slant of red earth planted with a variety of headstones and stark wooden crosses. The cemetery was at the far end of the main street and Preacher was watching a small procession approaching along the street, with sun-sparkled dust rising from beneath the wheels of the buckboard at the centre of the little group of walkers. On the buckboard was Bob Holbrook's coffin.

Dorcas sat on the seat, wearing a dark dress and sunbonnet. Beside her, at the reins was a lean stranger who had a range-hardened appearance and who smacked more than a little of the kind of gun-heavy ruffian who had recently shown up around Centro far too frequently. He held his right shoulder at an angle which suggested an injury.

If Preacher was suspicious of the young stranger, his suspicions were lessened by the fact that Doc Grogan walked beside the buckboard and behind him came a small string of homesteader men, women and children, almost the whole complement of those who had not fled in fear. Doc was known to be cautious about the company he was seen in, so Preacher figured the man at the reins did not lack respectability. He noted that none of the men in the funeral party carried guns — at least openly.

The buckboard halted at the cemetery gate. Preacher stepped forward and reached up to take Dorcas's hand in a tender grasp.

"May the Lord comfort you, Sister Dorcas," he said quietly. "May your days of grievin' be short. We knew our brother Bob to be a devoted brother an' a good neighbour. Be sure that the Lord, who knows us all far better'n we know ourselves understands his righteousness an' rewards him in His heavenly mansions."

139

"Thank you, Preacher," said Dorcas firmly. She was serious-faced and drawn, but bravely showed no sign of tears.

Preacher Weems produced his much-thumbed Bible from the pocket of his nondescript old coat and placed himself at the head of the group. They moved on through the gate and along the path between the graves.

Up on the buckboard, Dan Herrick stared stoically ahead. His shoulder still ached and his right arm was stiff and awkward. Out of respect for the occasion, he had shucked his shell-belt and holster and his Colt .45 was rammed into the waistband of his pants, but inside his shirt, well out of sight. He knew that Doc wore his own gun in its shoulder holster under his frock-coat.

The stiffness of his gun-hand worried him and, in collecting the coffin from the undertaker's premises and throughout their progression along the street, he and Doc kept wary watch for Walking C men. They might well come looking for retribution for his shooting Floyd and old Samuelson. He even wondered if McDade might have spurred decrepit old Marshal Yawberry into seeking him with a warrant for murder. On the other hand, he remembered that strange plea from the rancher about not wanting him killed. If Cal McDade did not want him shot, he would hardly attempt to have him hanged.

Then there was the matter of the conversation he had overheard in The Breaks. He figured McDade might have other things to contend with and, in that irksome way, the content of the conversation rose in his mind yet again. McDade had vipers in his own nest and didn't know it. Damned if he didn't feel concerned about the old fool!

The buckboard passed a huge granite memorial, by far the largest in the humble little cemetery. It was surmounted by a weeping angel, the sentimentality of which was contradicted by a carving of the Lone Star flag of Texas, crossed with the Stars and Bars of the Confederate States. The name 'McDade' was hammered out of the stone in big capitals. Plainly, Cal McDade had the tombstone created, perhaps somewhere further East, at considerable cost.

It had been erected since Herrick left this country and he realised that he was looking at the memorial to the girl he had loved. He gulped, remembering the miserable day when he and the other hands from the Walking C stood around a mere hole on that same spot, paying their last respects as the Major's daughter was lowered into her resting place.

He bit his lip as the wagon rumbled past the monument, noting that, Cal McDade, typically, had stamped his own personality even on this bleak place of the dead. The stone recorded that there lay his beloved Wife, Martha, who died so many years before and their beloved and treasured daughter,

Elizabeth ' . . . called to her rest in the flower of her youth . . . '

He noted that they were described as wife and daughter of ' . . . Calvin J McDade, sometime Major in the volunteer cavalry of the sovereign State of Texas, in the services of the Confederate States of America, during the struggle for the states' rights of the people of the South and sometime member of the military staff of Major General John Bell Hood, of Kentucky . . . '

The old ruffian seemed to have grabbed most of the space, even on the tombstone, as he wanted to grab the land around this region, thought Herrick with distaste. And, of course, his service in the great lost cause had to be emblazoned forth to the world.

The two Mexican peons who helped out around the cemetery had prepared the grave which yawned in the red earth. Some of the homesteader women gathered around Dorcas comfortingly and escorted her to the side of the grave while four of their men bore the coffin off the buckboard.

Herrick and Doc Grogan joined a small group of homesteader men standing to one side of the grave with their hats in their hands. Just as Preacher Weems took his place at the graveside and opened his book, two latecomers came walking along the pathway to join the burial group.

They were like two peas in a pod. Both were short and lean with bald heads and straggly whiskers. They wore long yellow duster coats and carried black, broad-brimmed hats. Both had the same walk, a peculiar, cat-like tread which was cautious, yet springy and lithe, though the pair were no longer young.

"The Candlin brothers, or at least two of them, Jacob and Samuel," murmured Doc to Herrick. "There's a third, Hosea, but he must be detained somewhere."

The identical Candlins paused beside Dorcas. "We're right sorry about your

144

trouble, Miss Dorcas. Hosea is, too. He can't be with us, but sends his condolences. We were all powerful proud to have Bob as a neighbour an' we respected him," said one of them. His accent was plainly from New England, a flat and almost toneless drawl.

"I know that, boys. Thank you," Dorcas replied with a small, appreciative smile.

Preacher Weems read a simple burial service and quoted a text on which he based a little homily which sought to show that, while the wicked appeared to prosper in the eyes of the world, it was the good and righteous man who truly triumphed in the end. It was a dignified procedure with none of Preacher's usual verbal fireworks. He obviously reserved such techniques for his attempts to bellow repentance out of those far gone in sin. In the course of the homily, the old evangelist made references to the certainty that those who lived by the sword would die by it.

The nods, grunts and subdued 'Amens' from the homesteaders indicated that they knew what he was getting at.

Afterwards, the party stood respectfully to one side while Dorcas spent a short time beside her brother's partially filled grave. Then a group of women escorted her back to the buckboard. She mounted with help from Herrick who then seated himself beside her and took the reins. He stole a glance at her and saw that, even in its grief and with moisture glistening on her cheeks, there was beauty in her face. It was the fresh, springtime beauty of a young woman who deserved joy and lightheartedness. Herrick felt a powerful urge to make it up to Dorcas, to somehow compensate her for the way she had been treated by the harsh men of this harsh land.

With the mourners walking behind it, the wagon rolled back along the cemetery path. Just outside the gate, Herrick halted it at Dorcas' request and she stepped down to thank and exchange handshakes with the homesteaders. Doc Grogan and the two Candlins drifted to the back of the gathering where they stood in a group which looked distinctly conspiratorial. Herrick joined them and, just as he did so, he noticed a familiar figure coming on horseback up the street, making for the funeral party.

It was one of the Walking C crew, a young fellow whom his lawman's eye had picked out in the group which had taunted Dorcas on the street and, again among those who cornered him in the ranch house. He had noted particularly his rawness and a demeanour which suggested he was not accustomed to such company and was unhappy in it.

The kid looked pretty much a tenderfoot. Still, looks could be deceptive. He was a Walking C man and there might be more of his kind around, looking for trouble.

The youngster halted his mount close to the funeral group, looked around and obviously spotted Doc Grogan. He came down from his saddle and led his animal over towards the medico. He walked with a noticeable limp.

"You Doctor Grogan?" he asked.

"I am," said Doc. "What can I do for you?"

"A man in town told me I'd find you up here, Doctor. I'm sorry to bother you at a time like this, but I wonder if you can find time to examine my leg. I think it might be broken."

"You ride for the Walkin' C, don't you, son?" put in Herrick.

"Used to. I quit," said the youngster in a shamefaced way. "I never rightly settled into the ways of the Major an' the bunch he has on his spread."

"How did you hurt the leg?" enquired Doc.

"Got throwed by my horse when I was tryin' to get out of the way of cows Mr Herrick here hazed back at us when we were chasin' him." He grinned at Herrick. "That was a right smart trick, Mr Herrick. I didn't particularly want to catch you. Matter of fact, I was glad when you got away. Was glad when you pulled that window trick, too."

"It was a pretty painful experience, young feller," grunted Herrick. "I'm only glad that beef didn't stampede all over you when you were thrown."

"Step aside here, son. I'll look at the leg here and now," said Doc.

Doc bent and asked the young wrangler to raise his aching leg into the air. He made him lower it and raise it three or four times then circle his foot around in the air. He felt the leg through the coarse fabric of the youngster's Levi's and questioned him about the nature and location of his pain.

Rising, the medico grunted: "There's no break there. Just a matter of a severe sprain and pulling of the muscles. Step down to my office in a minute or two and I'll strap the leg with a stout bandage. That'll make it easier for you to ride. Then when you get a chance to rest, give the leg some rest for a spell. A few days will put you right. I take it, from your packed warsack and saddle gear, you plan to ride some distance."

"Yes, sir, back to the family farm outside of Ogden, Utah. That's if my old man will have me back. I left in a kind of hurry after a few angry words with him."

"Ogden, Utah, huh? Same old tale of a Mormon boy who got tired of hard farm work and religious discipline, I guess. Figured maybe there was a brighter future outside for a young fellow who fancied he could make an impression on the world, 'specially since he thought he could use a gun pretty handily?"

"Well, that's about right, Doc," admitted the kid. "My name's Todd Calkins. I worked on a couple of spreads to the north of here an' got laid off when times got hard. I drifted down this way, fell in with a couple of rannihans who'd heard there were easy pickin's on the Walkin' C. They shared grub an' smokes with me on the trail, but I knew they were owlhooters. Never did rightly take to the goin's on at McDade's place, though. Lately, things are so much worse, I asked for my time and rode off the place. Do I owe you a fee, Doc?"

"No, young fellow, but you can help a little by telling Mr Herrick and myself more about what's going on at the Walking C."

"Well, it's become plumb peculiar in the last couple of days, Doc. The Major has gone awful subdued an' it seems like Ed Terry an' that fancy gunslinger, Pendexter, are really callin' the tune. It appears to me the Major is scared of 'em. As if they're kind of holdin' somethin' over him. I never did take to either of 'em, anyway. Both of 'em always hang back from anythin' the rest of the crew're up to an' that Pendexter, with his big reputation, behaves real superior to the other bunch. Everyone is plain scared of him an' that big Navy Colt."

"Looks like that pair are really drivin'

the wagon, now," observed Herrick to the medico.

Doc rubbed his chin thoughtfully. "Tell me this, son, did a little fellow name of Cory show up on the place, — a lawyer out of Tucson?" he asked.

"No, Doc. Can't say I met anyone of that kind. Fact is, there's more leavin' that outfit this last couple of days than are comin' to the spread. Terry an' Pendexter have been layin' down the law, sayin' they want real wranglin' work out of the crew. Anyone who came for easy pickin's can pack up an' leave. That's what made it easier for me to quit. A lot of 'em are headin' for Old Mexico because they face warrants in various states an' territories. The Walkin' C was only a last refuge on the way to the border for most of 'em, anyway. Like that pair they claim you shot, Mr Herrick. Floyd an' old Samuelson had Texas hangin' warrants against 'em. I heard it said they got out of Texas only a couple of hops ahead of the Texas Rangers."

Herrick gave a grunt of satisfaction. He had killed the pair in a straight case of self-defence but there were no witnesses to the event. Now, he knew it was unlikely that, at some future date, the law would visit retribution on him for the deaths of two who were being pursued by the Rangers for murder.

The two identical Candlin brothers had detached themselves from the funeral group and stood behind Doc Grogan, silently witnessing the young wrangler's tale. Now and then, they glanced at the doctor with a certain unfathomable glitter of their eyes the only spark of expression of life on their frozen, beard-tangled faces.

"Tell you what, son. You ride down to my office and I'll join you later to strap up that leg," instructed Doc. The youngster limped off to his animal.

Again, Doc rubbed his chin in his sage way and looked at Herrick. "Seems like things are falling to bits over yonder on Walking C grass, Dan. Terry and Pringle making their play to run the place, holding McDade bulldogged and running off the rannihans who only signed up for gun-wages in the old man's cockeyed war on the homestead folk. Next thing we know, they have signed a respectable crew and they'll be powerful cattle-barons. Of course, the Major might well have met with some strange fatal accident by that time. There'll be nobody to raise any dust about the legality of the way in which those two came by the title of the place, that's for sure. Could be that things are going our way and it'll soon be time to act."

Herrick looked around to make sure that none of the funeral party, gathered around Dorcas and talking in a subdued way, overheard him. "Now, c'mon, Doc," he urged. "You *are* plannin' somethin'. What do you mean by 'act'? You've been keepin' me in the dark for too long."

"Well, you had a bad shaking up, son. I wanted you to get over the experience fully before we really got down to cases. Even now, that arm and shoulder are far from what they should be. It's just a matter of that good citizenship President Arthur was talkin' about some time back, the stuff he claimed would be good for Arizona. Seems like Bob's death kind of dictates that we really do something for good and all."

"We?" queried Herrick.

"Well, these two gents and myself," answered Doc, indicating the Candlins. "And, knowing the kind of man you are, I don't believe you'd wish to be left out. I'm referring to what I mentioned before: a big battle to end a war. Maybe that's pitching it too high, though. More like a decisive skirmish than a big battle perhaps."

"With these two gents?" gasped Herrick, looking at the Candlin brothers, in their incongruous duster coats and with their ageing, bearded faces. They looked so much the quiet homesteader kind, he could not imagine them being involved in gun-action which was plainly what the enigmatic doctor was talking about.

"I should have said 'three gents'," corrected Doc. "Their brother, Hosea, at present otherwise engaged, will be in on it, too."

"Don't let it faze you none, Mr Herrick," said one of the Candlins, in his flat New England tones, "but we know what we're about. We don't shout about it because it's all long gone by, but us three brothers were once with Sheridan's Scouts."

Herrick stiffened. "Sheridan!" he exclaimed. "Sheridan!" This time, he spat out the name like a curse.

"Sure. Long ago, when we were all young."

To Confederates and their kin, the name of Philip H Sheridan, Lincoln's thrusting little Irish general, was almost as odious as that of William Tecumseh Sherman, whose vast army ravaged Georgia and reduced the city of Atlanta to a cinder.

Sheridan led a blue-coated tide in

156

a storm of destruction along the lush valley of the Shenandoah in Virginia with rich fields, full barns and fat livestock. Phil Sheridan's commander in the field, General U S Grant, gave him an instruction: "Make it so even a crow crossing that valley will have to carry his own rations." Little Phil's horde did it, fiercely resisted all the way by a Confederate army rapidly being squeezed of its lifeblood. Farms were levelled, crops destroyed and stock butchered.

Ahead of his scourge, Sheridan sent his squad of scouts, specially chosen for their knowledge of wild places. They wore Southern uniforms, infiltrated enemy camps, joined Rebel soldiers at their campfires to share tobacco, coffee and gossip. Then they melted back into the tangles of the valley to report to Sheridan. Under the rules of war, they ran the risk of being hanged as spies if caught by the enemy while in their uniform and some were.

Dan Herrick was no bigot and not

given to hating. Nevertheless, he was a Texan, son of a staunch Texas Rebel. He was still a man of the South whose stomach turned at mention of Sherman, Sheridan and cross-eyed Ben Butler, who was held to have insulted all Southern womanhood.

And here he was, hobnobbing with men who were once Sheridan's Scouts.

Doc Grogan grinned. "As Samuel says, Dan, don't let it faze you. Every man has a past. Every man is one thing at one stage of his life and maybe something else quite different at another stage."

"Yep. Peaceful farmers is all we are now," drawled the second brother. "That's all we ever wanted to be. We were raised in the piney woods of Maine an' could track an' trap before we could read. That's why the little general chose us for a special job. Never did anythin' to be ashamed of, though. What we did was done because we were strong Union men in the service of the Union. We knew

158

the Southern boys were just as earnest for their cause as ourselves an' we never hated 'em. We gave 'em a helpin' hand when we could. We understood 'em. After all, our mother was an Alabama girl an' as fine a belle as ever came out of the South. An' you know we were chancin' just by bein' in Rebel uniform."

Herrick gave a non-committal grunt. Sheridan's Scouts the strange Candlin brothers might have been, but that surely spoke for their skills and devotion to what they saw as duty. Such men were good allies, even if they were Yankees, he had to concede.

But allies in what? Doc was playing his old game of talking in generalisations with his allusions to a big battle to end a war. It was high time, he figured, to get down to brass tacks with Doc.

Turning to the medico, he began: "Now, see here, Doc. These plans you've been makin' . . . "

"All in good time, Dan. Right now, I have a patient waiting for attention

159

down at my office. You must excuse me. Anyway, Dorcas seems to want your attention," cut in Doc. "I'll see you later."

The funeral party was breaking up, with the few homesteader folk making for their buckboards and horses, tied up down the street. Dorcas had just said her farewells and was walking towards Herrick. Under the brim of her sombre bonnet, her quiet smile shone briefly when she looked at him and he felt the surge of admiration for her which he first knew when he witnessed her spirited behaviour on first encountering her on Centro's single street.

"Thank you for everything, Dan," she said huskily. "You helped me get through this morning."

Herrick shrugged. "I only drove the wagon, Dorcas. I'd be happier if it hadn't been necessary."

"You were a tower of strength. Just being by my side when we brought poor Bob on his last journey made you a tremendous comfort to me. And, last night, when I might have spent a night totally alone with my grief, you were a comfort just by being under the same roof."

Herrick nodded gravely, remembering the night. He had lain in Bob's bed, still plagued by pain in his arm and shoulder, dozing now and again but keeping his hand close to the Colt under the pillow. Maybe, just maybe, the Walking C rannihans would track him down to the homestead.

And, all night, he heard the girl's subdued sobbing from her room nearby. But, now, she was continuing the brave show she had put up all morning. Dorcas was a girl in a million. A girl who should be cherished.

He suddenly thought of Elizabeth, under that monument back in the cemetery. It was hard to imagine that anything of the essential being of Elizabeth lay beneath that huge stone, with its strident bombast concerning her father's military career. Again, he reflected that her smiles, twinkle-eyed lightheartedness and glowing kindness — everything making up what the Navajo would call her lingering *chindi* — could only be in the wide skies, clean air and brilliant sunshine. And he wondered what this essence of his beloved Elizabeth would make of the undeniable fact that he now felt stirrings of something close to what he felt for her when he considered the courageous Dorcas.

"Dan, you will come back to the homestead and stay at least until your shoulder and other wounds are fully healed, won't you?" continued Dorcas. "You're a welcome guest." Reaching out and laying her hand lightly on his sleeve, she added: "And I know you're to be trusted."

Herrick smiled. "That's kindly of you, Dorcas. Guess it won't harm these fool cuts of mine to help out with a few chores around the place. And I'll never add to your unhappiness while under your roof." He laid a meaningful emphasis on the last part of the statement.

A rumbling cough came as an interjection to remind him that the Candlin brothers still stood behind him.

"Samuel an' me will be gettin' along, Miss Dorcas," said Jacob. "We're right sorry we had to be with you in such unhappy circumstances but if you ever need a hand, just send word an' we'll come runnin', all three of us."

"Thanks, boys. You're good neighbours," she murmured. She shook hands with each brother in turn and each Candlin gave Herrick a parting nod.

"Reckon we'll be seein' you in due course, Mr Herrick," said Jacob.

"Reckon you will — in due course," returned Herrick.

And he escorted Dorcas back to the buckboard.

★ ★ ★

163

Azell Cory, attorney-at-law, was in a foul mood.

He was hot, sweaty and on horseback. He was also in a landscape which was little short of wilderness and he yet had many miles to go.

Time was when Mr Cory had been a young horseback lawyer in the rocky fastnesses of Colorado. He had enjoyed life back in those days and had learned much among the roaring, pioneer silver camps where a fortune might be made — or lost — within an hour. These days, however, he preferred to ride his fine chestnut around the streets of Tucson, where his one-man, somewhat secretive practice was established. He liked to ride for pleasure and at a gentlemanly pace. Riding under this merciless sun in a near-forgotten portion of Arizona Territory was quite another matter and a downright uncomfortable one. Furthermore, he was not sure such travelling was doing his fine chestnut any good.

Mr Cory could, however, take some satisfaction from knowing that, when it was all over, with the business fully attended to and certain papers now in his saddle pannier signed and witnessed, there would be rewards for him. They might not be rewards of which many brother lawyers, with their almost religious zeal for duty, would approve. But they would be quite acceptable within Mr Azell Cory's peculiarly drawn-up code of personal ethics.

For, in those Colorado mining camps, Mr Cory had learned certain twists and tangles in the law which a man might use to make his pocketbook grow fatter. After all, the camps were far from the big cities where lawyers formed themselves into coteries and societies, all devoted to preserving the good standing of a profession which the common man maligned all too readily.

Much use of those twists and tangles had gone into creating the terms in the papers which the lawyer was now carrying to the Walking C Ranch on this stretch of the journey after he and his mount had travelled by train from Tucson to the railhead at Benson, the chestnut being accommodated in the freight car. Cory hoped he had not been too closely observed either leaving Tucson or arriving in sweltering, desert-encircled Benson.

Now, he was riding an ill-defined, shaly trail, stirring puffs of dry dust. Two sun-punished slants of land shouldered up on either side of the trail which, just ahead of Cory, took a blind turn to the left. Cory, wearing a grey, frock-coated suit already reddened by dust, and a black broad-brimmed hat, had buckled a shell-belt around his middle and bore a holstered Colt .45 close to the centre of his vest, within easy reach. It was true that the Apache warriors no longer raided but a traveller had to take precautions in this country. There were owlhooters and road-agents, out of work cowhands and a whole variety of gun-heavy gents, all with less subtle means of fattening their wallets than those employed by Azell Cory, attorney-at-law.

Just as Cory urged his mount around the shoulder of land to his left, his heart leaped in alarm. He nudged the Colt loose in its holster.

Sitting on a dun pony on the trail ahead of him was a peculiar looking fellow who might well be one of the gentry Cory had no desire to meet. His animal was halted beside the trail and he was watching the lawyer approach with great interest.

He was a man of smallish stature, wearing a grimy yellow duster coat of the kind made famous by the cantankerous Eastern editor Horace Greeley on his Western travels and a wide black sombrero. Most of his face was covered in a tangled beard from which jutted an unlighted corncob pipe. Cory looked at the rider through narrowed eyes and gave the butt of his Colt another sly

167

nudge. There was no telling what weapons a man might conceal under such a garment as a long duster coat.

The rider thumped his pony with his knees, causing it to amble towards Cory. Neither seemed to be in any hurry, appearing to be fully geared to the slow pace demanded by such a broiling day.

"Well, now, here's a stroke of good fortune. An answer to a good man's prayer one might say if given to the study of religion," hailed the rider in a flat accent. "I'm right glad to see you, friend. Right glad to see a man who appears civilised."

The pair rode on to meet each other. Cory could see that the other was no longer young. Such of his face as was visible between shading hat-brim and matted beard was weatherbeaten and wrinkled but his dark eyes looked remarkably keen. The lawyer was relieved that the man on the pony was not presenting a loaded weapon with demands for cash and valuables — at least, not yet.

"Yes, sir. Right glad to see someone who looks as if he might be a man who appreciates tobacco," continued the rider, speaking around his wobbling corncob. "Would you have the means of lightin' a pipe about you?" He reined up just in front of the lawyer who also halted his mount.

"Why, yes," answered Cory cautiously, wondering if this was not merely an opening gambit leading to more sinister play. "As it happens, I relish a good cigar and I have a flint lighter in my pocket."

"You are a Samaritan, sir, beggin' your pardon if you consider that an irreverent thing to say," declared the bearded one. "I have such a device myself an' right handy it is — except when I'm fool enough to leave it behind me. Just been visitin' a neighbour back yonder an' stopped to give the old cayuse a breather an' take smoke. Filled up my pipe an' all then found I'd left the lighter back at my neighbour's place."

Azell Cory handed over his lighter. He was fully satisfied now that this was an eccentric old character who was totally harmless. The man in the duster clicked a flame out of the heavy flint-and-wheel device, applied it to the bowl of his pipe and sent up clouds of pungent smoke. He gave a deep sigh of satisfaction and returned the lighter. He took three or four puffs of the pipe then said: "You'll be ridin' straight ahead, I take it, sir?"

"I am," said the lawyer.

"Then I figure you won't mind if I ride with you some of the way. I turn off the trail to the left to my place. A simple settler on a little land grant is all I am. You, I take it, will be a drummer, though I don't see any samples. This is a hard way for a salesman to be journeyin'. It used to be better when the old stage was runnin' betwixt Benson an' Centro but

170

Centro got so danged run-down, the line stopped it."

"No, I am not a travelling salesman. I am an attorney," responded Cory haughtily. At once, he regretted it. It was said out of professional pride and Cory wanted as few as possible to know of his journey to this back-end of the Territory. Indeed, he intended to circle Centro by way of an obscure trail for the people of tiny towns had a way of noting strangers who passed through.

The man in the duster shrugged and puffed his pipe reflectively. "Well, drummer, lawyer or man workin' the land, I reckon it's all an honest livin' in the end," he observed at length.

A faint trail angled away to one side, becoming lost in the cactus-studded land.

"Reckon we part company here, sir. This here is the trail I take," nodded the pony-rider. "Right gratified to have met you an' thanks for the light."

"Good day to you," replied Cory, grateful that this encounter in such a

171

lonesome place had brought him no harm. The man in the duster was soon lost in the humps of land, boulders and cactus and Azell Cory continued straight ahead.

Just out of sight, Hosea Candlin halted his pony and patted its head. "Well, that was plumb interestin', wouldn't you say?" he asked the animal. "Mr Cory is on his way to the Walkin' C."

From beneath his duster coat, he brought forth a large watch on a heavy chain and consulted it thoughtfully. At length, he murmured: "It's certain he'll bypass Centro because he's too easily noticed. He took damn' good care not to tell me his name, but them initials 'AC' on his pannier were enough for me. So, allowin' on him takin' a few false trails an' restin' once in a while, he'll be at McDade's outfit soon after nightfall. I figure to-morrow night will be just right for our big thing. From my observations last night, the moon'll be just about right, too."

172

Hosea spurred his mount gently forward and chuckled deep in his beard. He was beginning to enjoy this situation mightily.

Two days before, his brothers had attended the funeral of their neighbour, bushwhacked because he clearly had the potential to ramrod intelligent resistance to the deviltry unleashed by McDade's half-baked war against the settlers. Since then, Hosea had pressed old skills into use. Knowing the time the daily train from Tucson arrived at Benson, he had planted himself among the boulders on one of the slants of land shouldering the trail. Inside his deceptive duster coat were a supply of iron rations, a big desert water canteen and a spyglass.

Hosea, the old Sheridan Scout, kept as tight a watch on the trail as any he kept in the Shenandoah campaign. The first day was fruitless but the second gave him a view of Cory approaching, whereupon Hosea made his appearance at the side of the trail as an amiable and eccentric nester in need of a light.

As the youngest of the three brothers, he had volunteered for the lookout duty right after Doc Grogan had made a late night call at their homestead. He was now mighty pleased that he had not lost any of his prowess at observation and deception.

Yes, sir, he thought, he and his brothers were pretty clever back in the days when they scouted well ahead of little Phil Sheridan's army, mingling with Rebels and deceiving them with accurate impersonations of the Alabama accent employed by their Southern mother.

They were interesting times, he thought with a chuckle, heading for the Candlin homestead.

And, now that Cory was in this country, it looked like there were more interesting times just over the hill.

8

DORCAS came out of her small homestead kitchen into the sunshine.

All morning, she had heard Dan Herrick chopping and stacking cordwood at the back of the house. There was no immediate need of wood fuel with summer just about to open, but Herrick said he wanted to earn his keep and the exercise would limber up his injured shoulder and arm. It worried him that his right arm had a way of seizing up now and again. Dorcas remembered that speedy draw and gunfighter's crouch the day he defended her against McDade's ruffians and knew why the state of the arm concerned him. Diplomatically, she never mentioned his obvious skill with a gun. She liked the tall, rugged and yet strangely gentlemanly guest under her roof and it worried her that, like so many men in this untamed land, he had the potential for violence — only, in him, it had been tamed to a controlled and measured violence. It had to do with calculation and trigger-skill. It was almost an art.

Now, the sound of Herrick at work had ceased and, as the girl walked around the side of the house, she saw why. Herrick was standing beside a pile of cordwood. He had buckled on his gun-gear unknown to Dorcas and now he was honing up that fast draw, unholstering the gun and levelling it a clump of shrubbery across the yard at lightning speed.

Dorcas stood at the side of the shack, watching him with her heart in her mouth. She thought: *Guns and violence, slaughter and wanton killing. It was so much a part of what men so grandly boasted was the code of the West. When would it ever stop? Maybe the homesteaders who had quit were right. They only wanted a quiet life. Maybe she was right to think of quitting* herself. *Even this curiously gentle man who was so manifestly intelligent and who rose to defend her when she was alone in the midst of danger had a reservoir of violence within him. Now, he was demonstrating how keenly he had made a craft of it. She hoped it would never overwhelm him and finally consume him. For he was special . . . so very special . . .*

Herrick said: "Not so bad, eh, Dorcas? The arm is gettin' back to normal, more or less. Still a bit stiff, but not so bad on the whole." The fact that he said it without turning indicated that he knew she was there, although she was behind him. It was as if he had eyes in the back of his head. And that, too, was part of his gunfighter's skill, she thought.

He turned, holstering the sixgun and he smiled that spontaneous, bashful smile she liked so much. He rubbed the length of his right shoulder and arm with his left hand. "Not too bad on the whole," he repeated with satisfaction.

Dorcas knew there was a disturbing portent in his actions. She had not failed to note how Herrick and Doc Grogan got into a conspiratorial huddle almost as soon as Herrick returned to consciousness after his ordeal in the The Breaks. Something was in the wind and she knew it just as surely as a mother knew when her young sons were plotting mischief. She only hoped that, whatever it was, it did not bring more killing and mourning.

"I'm glad the arm is improving," she said. "I'm just about to fix coffee. Want some?"

"Sure," he said, grinning and wiping his brow.

Inside, he went to Bob's room which had become temporarily his own and unbuckled his gun-gear. Laying it on the bedside chair, he covered it with his slicker. He knew that the sight of weaponry offended Dorcas, the more so since Bob's violent death and he regretted not choosing a more remote spot in which to practise his draw.

178

In the kitchen, Dorcas had prepared coffee and the biscuits she baked so expertly. Herrick sat on one side of the rough deal table and Dorcas on the other. Their eyes met and they sat there without speaking but appreciating each other.

Dorcas thought again of his specialness. In so many ways, he was like Bob, seeming to understand her as a brother understood his sister. She wondered if Herrick felt anything more than brotherly sentiments towards her. There was no doubt that he was all man, strong, sinewy, tough and, doubtless, mule-stubborn man through every inch. Yet there was no lust in him, none of that leering, glowing eyed and near slavering passion she had seen and sensed in so many men of the frontier. Instead, he had a natural gentleness and a courtesy which was probably the courtesy of the old South, for he had told her his family was from Texas. She knew she was safe with him and could sleep easily under the same roof.

Herrick finished his coffee and she poured him a second cupful, thinking how he appreciated coffee after a spell of hard work in just the way Bob had. He was like Bob in so many ways that he eased the emptiness left by her brother's death.

Nodding his thanks for the replenishment, Herrick savoured the coffee and commented: "Good coffee, Dorcas. An' your biscuits are as good as ever. You sure know how to treat a guest royally."

"Just honest and plain food, Dan," she smiled. "You're welcome to it any time."

"Not without givin' somethin' in return. So I reckon I'll go tend to the horses right after I finish this."

When he left the table, he strode back to the yard and Dorcas watched him go. She hoped that, after supper, they would sit around and talk for a spell, as they had the previous night. It was an experience which soothed the shock and hurt of Bob's brutal death

180

and the constant anxiety of living on the edge of danger in this beautiful but untamed place. She enjoyed his company because he was so refreshingly different from the run of men who lived on the frontier, packing a sixshooter as a matter of course.

Herrick mentioned that he was once a law officer a long way up north. She suspected that he did so to allay any lingering fears that he was so proficient at gunplay because of a lawless background.

He talked about his youth in Texas, about his decent folks and how his hard-working father turned Confederate soldier out of devotion to beliefs which caused so many otherwise peaceful men to take the path of war.

He never mentioned a past love but she suspected there might have been one at some time because he knew how to treat a woman with a quiet and straightforward courtesy but never showed embarrassing, overweening flattery.

She, in turn, mentioned her early life and her family's struggles and the way Bob had cared for her perhaps with even more devotion than a full brother would show. He was a man who put honesty and straight-dealing into the development of the West. He had wanted to go homesteading alone, but she had insisted on accompanying him. In her own way, she too was feeling the pull of the magnet of opportunity which was drawing new settlers into the Western lands so recently won from the Indian.

She had mentioned that she had some little experience of teaching school and might have to return to it somewhere in the East if she gave up the homestead. Herrick had reacted strongly to the suggestion.

"Don't quit, Dorcas," he advised. "Don't just give up an' run for it. You owe it to Bob to stay an' make your life out here. Both of you put too much work into creatin' this place. Arizona Territory needs women like you. You're too darned spirited to become just another meek schoolma'am away to the East. You have the kind of strength an' courage needed to make this country decent an' civilised. It'll all be tamed much faster than you imagine. Just hang on awhile and see."

The words had a powerful and heartfelt ring to them. But, still, she was in doubt. She and Bob came out here with high, sunny hopes and now Bob lay in the red shale of Centro's cemetery.

Again and again, her thoughts turned to the way Herrick had put in practice with his gun arm.

Meanwhile, Herrick busied himself in the stable, feeding and grooming his own bronc and the animals used by Dorcas to draw her buckboard. There ought to have been a third animal housed there, the saddle horse which Bob had been riding when ambushed. If turned loose by Terry and Pringle, the gunfighter, after the killing, it had not wandered back to its home. Possibly it had been discovered by someone who simply stole it but, more likely, the bushwhackers took it out to the desert wastes and callously shot it. Diplomatically, he never mentioned the horse to Dorcas, nor did he tell her he knew the identity of Bob's killers.

They had supper, but Dorcas was denied the quiet evening chat with her guest afterwards.

Just as they finished coffee, Herrick sat up, suddenly intent. The clatter of horses sounded outside and a voice called out the traditional Western "Hello, the house!" It was unmistakably that of Doc Grogan. Dorcas felt a qualm of unease at hearing it. Amiable and upstanding Doc, that pillar of a community badly lacking in such pillars, could create misgivings in her now that she had witnessed the conspiratorial side of him. And she needed no telling that he and Herrick were plotting something.

Herrick opened the door. It was dark outside, with the sky now and then but faintly lit by a thin sliver of late-month moon, a fugitive among slowly drifting clouds. Doc was reined up in the yard. He was dressed in dark clothing and there were three riders with him. In the fitful light, he saw that they were the Candlin brothers, with their familiar Horace Greeley dusters now replaced by similar long overcoats of black.

"I brought the Candlin boys, Dan," called Doc. "Can we have a few quiet words together, maybe in private — possibly in the stable, so we don't disturb Dorcas?"

Dorcas appeared in the lamplight, standing in the doorway behind Herrick. This was trouble, she thought. The doctor, the Candlin brothers and Herrick were hatching some kind of plot and Bob's death was the catalyst which had set it off. She knew that these five were about to plunge into yet more violence. She did not want more violence and she did not want any of these five decent men to suffer through it. But, most of all, her fears were for

Dan Herrick. Womanlike, however, she knew that it was nigh impossible to stop men in their tracks once they were intent on some headlong action.

At the sight of her, the new arrivals twitched their hatbrims.

"Evening, Dorcas," said Doc. "Just called on Dan for a chat. We won't bother to come in. Out here will do fine."

Dorcas bowed to the inevitable. They were set upon their scheme, whatever it was, and there was no stopping them. "No, come on in and have some coffee. I'll leave you chat in peace," she said.

They trooped into the homestead, holding their hats, looking like sheepish schoolboys. Dorcas invited them to sit around the table then went out to replenish the coffee pot.

"We figure to-night will be right for our big thing," declared Doc in a low tone.

Herrick gave a tight grin. 'Big thing', he knew, was Civil War talk, used by both sides to indicate a forthcoming battle.

"You mean your battle to finish a war, eh, Doc? Well, high time, too. You've been hedgin' around all my questions an' keepin' me in the dark for too long."

"I wanted to be certain that arm of yours is in reasonable condition because we'll have gunplay, that's for sure," apologised Doc. "I also had to be sure we played everything just right and now, everything is in place. It will have to be to-night because that twisted lawyer Cory has just about arrived at McDade's spread with the papers to put it into the possession of Pringle and Terry. To-night, the whole bunch of us will raid the Walking C and put a stop to it."

A couple of throaty chuckles sounded across the table and Herrick saw the bearded Candlins grinning in the lamplight. All three of the old Sheridan Scouts were plainly enjoying this situation.

"Of course, we're assuming you want to have a hand in it," Doc continued.

"Come on, Doc," countered Herrick. "You know damn' well I'm with you all the way. You've been plottin' this move like some field commander, haven't you, you crafty old snake!" The blood was stirring in him now and he was beginning to relish the prospect of action as much as the grotesque Candlins.

"It was done with invaluable help from these old Phil Sheridan ruffians," admitted Doc. "But that was only the planning stage. We have to get the whole thing in the bag. And, as I just warned you, it'll come to gunplay."

Automatically, Herrick rubbed his arm and shoulder and flexed the fingers of his right hand. Dorcas re-entered, bringing fresh coffee and the five fell silent. *Mischievous boys*, she thought again as she observed their huddled forms around the table. That was exactly what they reminded her of and, once more, her fervent hope was that they were not about to plunge into some disastrous enterprise.

When she had departed, Herrick asked: "What's the strength of the opposition out at the Walkin' C, Doc?"

"It's depleted a little more because I saw a bunch of riders going through Centro this afternoon. I guess more of them are asking for their time now that Terry and Pringle are playing a heavy hand."

"Yeah, — Pringle," drawled Herrick slowly.

From beneath his all-concealing black coat, Jacob Candlin produced a square of paper and a lead pencil and shoved them across the table.

"Dan, do you remember the layout of the bunkhouse up yonder? Could you draw a plan of it? Y'know, showin' where the door is, an' how the windows are placed an' the way the bunks are arranged an' what kind of space there is so a couple of fellers might move around in the dark if they had a clear idea of it in their minds?"

Herrick took up the pencil. "Well, it's a few years since I was in there but, unless it's been altered, there's only one door, the bunks are in two rows, one atop the other, along each wall . . . " He started to draw and Jacob and Samuel watched intently, giving occasional nods and grunts.

When they rose from the table Herrick, flexing the fingers of his gunhand again, had the feeling that, at last, he was on his way to some decisive action about the situation on these ranges. After all, his first visit to the Walking C ended in his taking some severe punishment, although he could take some comfort from knowing that it also led to his discovering who lay at the heart of the deviltry hereabouts.

But, this time, Elizabeth, it's goin' all my way, he thought. *I'm goin' in smokin' an' they won't get their hands on your old man's outfit.*

The five prepared to leave with a carefully hammered out plan in mind. Herrick went to Bob's room, found a dark shirt and black buckskin vest in his warsack, changed into them and buckled on his gun-gear. Dorcas was waiting at the door when he walked out. She looked serious faced at his holstered .45 and the outfit which indicated dark-of-the-moon riding.

Doc Grogan and the Candlins took in the glances exchanged by Herrick and the girl and Doc called hastily: "We'll be moving off, Dorcas. Thanks for the coffee and your hospitality."

"So, you're going off on some wild scheme of yet more violence and killing, as if there hadn't been enough already," said Dorcas huskily.

"We don't want it that way, Dorcas. But others do an' we have to stop 'em once an' for all before they overwhelm this country an' destroy anythin' that's halfway honest an' decent."

She bit her lower lip and turned her head away. "Don't get killed or hurt," she said, obviously fighting against tears. "Just don't get killed." She grasped the sleeves of his shirt

191

and tugged it. "I'll never stop you, I know that. You're like a bunch of kids who get into any kind of trouble without thinking but, for God's sake, come back safely — all of you."

He put a hand on each of her shoulders and squeezed them gently.

"We did plenty of thinkin' about it," he said quietly. "An' we'll all come back safely."

He strode away towards the door quickly. Outside, he found Doc and the Candlins already mounted up. He noted three dark shapes of some outsized weapons in scabbards slanted against the saddles of the brothers and squinted against the darkness to identify them.

"They look like Sharps buffalo guns," he said on an incredulous note.

"Sure. That's exactly what they are," returned one of the shadowy brothers. "We did some buffalo huntin' after the war. Little Phil Sheridan signed us up when he led that party of European noble folks on the plains. These beauties are Sharps 40-65-330's."

"You wouldn't use one of those weapons on a man would you?"

Another Candlin chuckled. "Only if push came to shove, but the sight of 'em can sure throw a powerful scare into a feller."

Herrick moved off to the stable to saddle his bronc. He shuddered, thinking of the effect on a man which something so powerful as a Sharps rifle, specially created to drop a lumbering buffalo, could have. The grotesque Candlins were obviously more desirable as allies than enemies.

The door of the homestead remained firmly closed as if Dorcas had no wish to witness their departure. Then, just as they clattered away, Herrick turned his head and saw the curtain at the lamplit window twitch back.

He was aware of her anxious gaze following them as they rode into the night.

9

CLOUDS banked high in the acres of desert sky, masking the thin moon, as the five reached Walking C grass. They kept a steady pace, avoiding the normal approach by way of the ranch road. Guided by Herrick, they made a semicircular ride so they would come upon the ranch house from the rear.

Herrick, remembering how McDade had earlier planted lookouts, kept a wary eye on the shrouded terrain for signs of distant riders or glimmerings of fires indicating the night camps of such sentinels. None were seen. Terry and Pringle had probably so far usurped McDade's authority over the outfit that his writ no longer ran. The rancher's fevered notion that armies of sodbusters were about to invade his graze doubtless accounted for his posting the lookouts

194

but Terry and Pringle had probably withdrawn them. Furthermore, the reports of the Mormon youngster and Doc Grogan concerning an exodus of hired gunnies indicated depleted manpower on the spread. Hence, the party's unimpeded progress so far.

The riders crested a rise and came quickly down it so as to be skylined only briefly. The ranch headquarters lay below them, lamplight yellowing the big rear window through which Herrick had escaped.

They rode cautiously into a small grove of live oaks, tethered their animals to branches then went cautiously ahead on foot. Almost in the yard, Herrick hissed a warning and made a downward sweep with his arm. The five dropped to the earth and watched the yard, where Herrick had spotted a dark figure and a tiny red light, periodically glowing brighter.

"Someone takin' a smoke," he grunted. "Hopefully, he's about ready to turn in."

195

They hugged the earth closely, trying to pierce the darkness to discover whether the man was alone. So far as could be discerned, he was. Eventually, they saw the glow of the cigarette die and heard the man in the yard hawk and spit. The distant sound of his feet, moving off to the gallery of the bunkhouse rode on the still air, followed by the creak and slam of the door. The raiders watched the lamplight window of the bunkhouse until the light finally winked out.

"Last of McDade's gunnies safely in his blankets and bound for dreamland," whispered Doc.

"Yeah, an' Samuel an' me'll give 'em the nightmare of their lives," chuckled Jacob Candlin. Like his brothers, he carried his big buffalo hunting rifle and he hugged it to himself meaningfully.

"Listen, boys, we all know what we have to do, every man to his own job but, don't forget, when it comes to facin' Pringle, leave him to me," warned Herrick. "He's sheer poison an' he's the one who'll give us real trouble."

Crouching, they ran forward and reached the yard where Jacob and Samuel detached themselves from the group, hastened off towards the bunkhouse and dropped to the ground in the shadow of its wooden wall. There, they drew off their boots, abandoned them and, with Sharps rifles clutched against their bodies, crept silently forward like black-coated ghosts. Without a sound, they mounted the bunkhouse gallery and moved towards the door.

Herrick, Doc and Hosea moved directly to the back of the ranch house.

They dropped into the darkness beneath the lamplit, uncurtained back window, the damage to which had been temporarily repaired by a board nailed across a section of broken panes. Enough panes remained vacant of glass, however, to allow angry voices to drift out into the night.

"Damned old fool! Why don't he wake up? I didn't hit him all that hard," came a breathless and anxious jittering. "I'll hit him again if he don't wake soon." Herrick recognised the voice as that of Terry, the foreman.

"Don't be so damned stupid. You hit him too hard in the first place. He's an old man, how much pistol-whipping do you think he can take?" This time, it was the smooth, Eastern educated voice of Larry Pringle, the long-haired gunfighter who preferred to be known as Lafe Pendexter.

"Yes, take it easy. How do you expect him to sign if you beat him to death?" objected a voice unknown to Herrick but surely that of the Tucson lawyer, Azell Cory. "Give him a chance to recover. If his signature is too shaky, it'll be obvious he signed under duress."

"They've pistol-whipped McDade, but it sounds like he hasn't signed anything," whispered Herrick. "Terry sounds good an' mad. I only hope

198

they don't kill the old fool. So far, he's held out."

He unwound from his crouching position, removed his hat to make himself less significant, stood on tiptoe and looked through a corner of the window.

McDade was slumped in an armchair with his head drooping forward and Herrick could make out a crimson splotch on it. Terry stood over him, dark-faced with anger and holding a sixgun. Beside the foreman was a small man whose garb suggested he was more at home in legal offices and courtrooms. Leaning languidly against a table in the background was Larry Pringle. As usual, he appeared aloof from the activities around him, as if they were all somewhat beneath him. The lamplight put a dull glitter on his big Navy Colt and tell-tale longhorn buckle. On the table were several papers with an ink bottle from which a pen slanted.

Herrick crouched again and reported

what he saw to his companions.

"Come on," whispered Doc, asserting his remarkable talent for generalship. "Let's act before Terry harms McDade any further. He's obviously going off half-cocked."

"An', remember, Pringle is mine," cautioned Herrick.

They crept towards the front of the house, mounted the gallery and went soft-footed to the door.

At the bunkhouse, only seconds before, the door was noiselessly opened by the two bootless Candlins. Like two sombre-coated ghosts, they slipped into its black interior, recalling the layout from Herrick's drawing. They closed the door without a sound and waited. Then, deliberately, Samuel cleared his throat with a harsh rasping.

In the dense darkness, somebody stirred and mumbled sleepily: "Hey! Who's there? Who just came in?"

Out of the pitch black, Samuel bellowed: "We did, friend, a whole bunch of us — an' all armed with

200

Sharps buffalo pieces. Lie still like you were frozen solid if you don't want to be pulped into dog meat." Immediately, he dropped into a crouch and crept noiselessly forward, flattened himself against a far wall and, in a dramatically altered voice, growled: "That's right. We'll be right happy to cut loose on you if you try any shots in this direction."

"Sure, an' we, over this side, will enjoy doin' the same. We only have to hear the click of a hammer an' you've got yourselves an artillery barrage. Remember — Sharps' buffalo guns!" growled Jacob from the further side.

To the men in the bunks, there was no knowing how many intruders had infiltrated the darkness and were training high-calibre buffalo guns on them. Voices appeared to be coming from every direction around the door and there was no back door to the bunkhouse so it was impossible to chance slipping out of the blankets and sneaking out.

"You fellers, whoever you are, wouldn't really open up with buffalo guns, would you?" jittered one of the Walking C men.

"Well, now why don't you just try us?" invited Jacob from an entirely different angle and in a grating voice which made him sound like another man. "We're mostly mountain lion an' alligator an' we were raised on rattlesnake poison. Try sneakin' for your guns in the dark an' you'll think you're in the middle of the battle of Gettysburg."

The men in the bunks kept a scared silence.

"Don't try movin' until we say so," instructed Samuel.

A tight, fear-fraught silence settled on the darkened bunkhouse.

At a corner of the ranch house, Herrick and his companions were in a tight huddle. Herrick and Doc drew their sixguns.

"When we walk in off the gallery, we go right ahead to the door facing

202

us and that's the room they're in," whispered Herrick.

Doc nodded. "Good. We'll move through quickly. When we're inside their rooms, Hosea, you plant yourself by the door and cover the whole room with that artillery piece of yours. I'll tackle Terry and you, Dan — "

"Sure, — I'll deal with Pringle," finished Herrick.

They moved forward, mounted the gallery steps silently and crept ahead to the big front door. It swung open easily and the trio moved quickly into a large, semi-darkened room where only one oil-lamp burned in a far corner. Dead ahead was an open door from which light bloomed and voices issued.

"By God, I'll make him sign," Ed Terry was saying. There was a near hysterical, slightly insane note in his voice.

"And I keep telling you he'll be unable to sign if you keep beating him, you fool," came the voice of Azell Cory, which sounded even more agitated than the foreman's.

The three intruders moved in swiftly, Doc and Hosea showing remarkable agility for their years. At once, Hosea leaned against a door jamb and levelled his buffalo gun. Doc stood to one side of him with his Peacemaker on Terry who was standing in a startled arrested pose over McDade who was crouched in his chair. Over to the right, Larry Pringle, totally startled, hoisted his rump off the edge of the table behind him. But his hand remained well clear of his Navy Colt when he realised that the mouth of Herrick's gun was squarely covering him.

By God, he is gettin' old for sure," said a voice in Herrick's brain. *A few years ago, a man with his reputation would have sensed our presence before we got into the room and he'd meet us with a drawn gun.*

There was a sudden scuttling sound as Cory hastened behind a chair in a corner from where he surveyed the scene with an ashen face.

Ed Terry, his face twisted with anger, seemed to snap totally and appeared to blame McDade for the intrusion. In spite of the threat of Doc's Peacemaker, he lifted his gun menacingly over the rancher's head.

"You set us up for this, you lousy old skunk," he screeched. "You somehow fixed up a gun-trap for us. By God, nobody's stoppin' me at this stage. I'll beat your brains out. If anyone's gettin' killed around here, I'll make sure you are, too." He brought his arm higher, then began to swing the Colt down towards McDade's bleeding head.

Herrick, standing to one side of him, caught the action with the tail of his eye, took his gaze off Pringle for an instant and swung his .45 over in a swift arc to connect with Terry's skull before the foreman's blow struck. Terry gurgled, rocked drunkenly, then his legs buckled. He dropped his gun and fell like a sack of bricks at the feet of the huddled and still form of the rancher.

There was a speedy move from Larry Pringle which Herrick detected even before the foreman hit the floor. Herrick swung around quickly, arresting the gunfighter's lightning move. Pringle's hand jerked to stillness with the fingers almost grasping the butt of his holstered Navy Colt.

He's still pretty damned fast, declared the voice in Herrick's brain.

"It's the end of your trail, Pringle," Herrick stated flatly.

The gunfighter's face twitched at the mention of his correct name.

"You know too much," he said without emotion.

"Sure, I know your name as well as Judge Isaac Parker knew it when he wrote it on a hangin' warrant."

Larry Pringle gave a grating laugh. "Do you imagine you can put me on Parker's gallows over at Fort Smith while one of his mealy-mouthed parson friends preaches to the usual audience of yokels from Arkansas and Indian Territory on how another transgressor is about to reap the wages of sin?"

"It's no more than you have comin' for whatever you did in Indian Territory but particularly for bushwhackin' Bob Holbrook an' your part in Rogerson's killin'," responded Herrick. "I heard you were fast with a gun but straight accordin' to the rules. Seems you're gettin' old an' scared, though, an' you've forgotten the rules. You've turned to smart, thievin' schemes — an' to backshootin'."

Pringle's face hardened. "It's easy to talk with a gun in your hand, Herrick. Mostly, I figure you for a clown who's good at throwing himself through windows. I saw you draw in Centro, though, and you're fast all right. But just being fast means nothing until you slap leather against a man who just might be faster." The long-haired gunslinger paused and his eyes filled with a glowering, single-minded purpose. It was the stare he and Herrick had exchanged on the street in Centro. The challenge Herrick knew he could not duck.

Pringle's lips curled contemptuously under the well trained moustache, His eastern voice became a chilling, slow drawl.

"I'm saying, Herrick, that I can still outdraw you," he pronounced. "And I'm saying you're too damned yellow to put up your gun and slap leather against me according to those rules you keep harping on."

Herrick detected a stirring from both Doc and Hosea. Without turning and keeping his eyes locked with Pringle's, he warned: "Steady, boys. This is between him an' me."

He took a couple of swift, catlike steps back and dropped into a slight crouch. He quickly jammed his .45 back into its holster. Then he swung his arm away from it.

Immediately, Larry Pringle's hand streaked for his holstered Navy Colt. Herrick's hand moved with equal speed at exactly the same moment.

Then it jerked to a halt an inch away

208

from the butt of his gun, quivering into a frozen claw as pain seared like a burn from a branding iron through Herrick's shoulder and down his arm. He gave a sharp, involuntary gasp as he tried to clutch his gun butt. His arm and hand refused to respond.

He was aware of Pringle, grinning like the Angel of Death. His Navy Colt was clear of leather, levelling at Herrick.

Herrick thought madly that the gunfighter had called him a clown who threw himself through windows. By God, he was right. He was about to pay for that fool window trick with his life . . . and he'd promised Elizabeth that he'd prevent the theft of her old man's outfit . . . he was a fool, a clown . . . and a dead one at that . . .

He closed his eyes and a vision of two women swam into his mind: Elizabeth and Dorcas, both beautiful, tranquil and smiling.

Then a sixgun blast bellowed through the room like the crack of doom.

10

HERRICK felt no pain.

There was only a cold, anti-climactic shock washing through him.

He opened his eyes and found he was still upright and in a fog of gunsmoke. In the midst of it was Larry Pringle, standing like a soldier at attention with a look of utter surprise on his face. His eyes were as round as silver dollars, wide-open but unseeing. His arms were by his sides and the Navy Colt was just dropping from his right hand.

Abruptly, his mouth dropped agape and he began to topple forward like a felled tree. Herrick danced out of the way as the gunfighter's corpse hit the floor face down, the head only inches from his boots.

"Stinkin' thief!" growled the voice of Cal McDade.

Herrick turned to see McDade crouched in his armchair with a smoking Colt in his hand, — Ed Terry's weapon which had fallen from the foreman's hand when Herrick hit him. "Damned stinkin' thief!" spluttered McDade. "I took him on to ramrod a crew against sodbusters who aimed to steal my range an' he set about robbin' me instead. Him an' this other stinkin' thief!" He delivered a kick to the ribs of Terry, lying in front of his chair and showing signs of coming to.

Behind the chair in the corner, only the top of Azell Cory's head was visible and the lawyer was quivering like an aspen in a gale. Doc and Hosea were still covering the room, one with his Peacemaker and the other with his fearsome buffalo-slaying piece. Each gave Herrick a satisfied grin and an answering grin formed on Herrick's face as he began to fully appreciate what had happened.

McDade was plainly more conscious

than unconscious when Terry dropped at his feet and his gun fell close to the chair. He faked total unconsciousness until he had his chance to grab the foreman's sixgun and loose a shot at Pringle only a split second before the gunfighter triggered his weapon.

The rancher eased himself upright in the chair and brushed a trickle of blood away from his brow.

"Good thing you fellers busted in when you did," he muttered. "This lousy sidewinder, Terry, might have beaten me to death. I'm obliged to you for takin' a hand, Dan."

"You damned old fox. You dropped Pringle just before he dropped me," breathed Herrick. "I'm the one who has call to be obliged."

He motioned to the terrified Cory with the barrel of his Colt, making him emerge from the space behind the chair. On the floor, Ed Terry was groaning, holding his head and attempting to sit up.

Hosea Candlin, still leaning against

the jamb of the door, fished his corncob pipe from the pocket of his long black coat, shoved it into the midst of his beard then produced a heavy flint-and-wheel lighter from another pocket. He made a cheerful gesture with it in the direction of Azell Cory.

"Remembered to bring it along this time, Mr Cory," he grinned. "Won't have to trouble you for a light."

McDade spat the harsh taste of cordite from his mouth and Herrick saw with some satisfaction that he was suddenly looking much more his old self. In spite of the beating he had taken, he appeared to have had his old fire revived within him. The bellowing old Texan of the longhorn trails he was before his daughter's death quelled his feisty spirit was beginning to show through.

"By grab!" he spluttered. "My bacon saved by you, Dan — I figured you were dead someplace by now — an' by a damned scrubby old nester. An', you, Doc Grogan, — a near-sighted old sawbones. It's you bein' here I can't get over most of all!"

Hosea Candlin glowered at him. "I'll thank you not to call me a damned scrubby old nester, Major," he objected with heavy dignity. "I'll have you know I had the honour of servin' under General Philip Henry Sheridan — as one of his scouts in the Valley of the Shenandoah. I ain't alone, either, there's two more of us, who're busy in your bunkhouse right now. An' both of 'em old Sheridan Scouts."

"Sheridan! That monkey-shaped little Yankee ruffian had hands as bloody as the unhung murderer Sherman!" howled McDade.

"While on the subject, Major," interrupted Doc Grogan, "let me say that I'm not flattered by being called a near-sighted sawbones. Time was when I rode with John Singleton Mosby."

"Mosby!" the rancher exclaimed. "Hell, Doc, you were a guerrilla with the great Mosby? Mosby, the man who could bring his raiders out of nowhere, hammer the Yankees into a pulp an' disappear again. By grab, Mosby was a Southern soldier worth the name!"

Herrick stared at Doc with as much amazement as McDade. Now he understood Doc's prowess at organising undercover gathering of information, plotting dark-of-the-moon actions and his enthusiasm for what he called a big battle to end a war. He recalled how the medico once referred to calling on half forgotten skills. They were plainly the skills learned when he raided with the little grey ghost, John S Mosby. Hitherto, Doc had never given a hint as to where his allegiance lay in the war. Even his accent gave no clue as to his regional origins.

Mosby, no bigger than little Phil Sheridan, organised a network of cunning Southern partisans which raided and harried the forces of the North with hurricane speed and abruptness. Their activities turned whole swathes of northern Virginia into 'Mosby's Confederacy'.

Well and truly the old McDade now, the rancher chuckled. "You, a Mosby man, Doc? I'd never have believed it. Were you with him the time he captured that blasted Yankee general in bed?" His face suddenly darkened and he bestowed another glower on Hosea Candlin. "But associatin' with damned Sheridan Scouts! By God, that sticks in my craw, Doc — a Mosby man in the company of Sheridan Scouts! I don't know how you can do it."

Doc brushed back his moustache and gave the rancher a glare which almost cracked his glasses. "To save your skin and your spread, you ungrateful old fool. When are you going to stop fighting the big war? It's been over for twenty years. I probably don't venerate Abe Lincoln's name any more than you do, but at least I reckon the man was sincere when he said at the end of the war 'We are one people now'. That's how these gents and I acted — as one people, to help make a new country fit for peaceable folks to live in. These days, it doesn't matter what colour pants a man wore in the war. Can't you get that through your skull, you stubborn old horned toad?"

Herrick kept his sixgun levelled at the white-faced lawyer and quivering foreman and grinned.

"Cal, how about breakin' out your liquor bottle instead of arguin'?" he invited. "With the exception of these two, who deserve nothin' but what's comin' to 'em, some of us would appreciate a drink."

Herrick stepped out of the ranch house, leaving Doc, Hosea and McDade to guard the cowed lawyer and foreman.

The silver and gold of the desert dawn was beginning to brighten the sky. By its light, he saw a somewhat comical tableau lining up on the bunkhouse gallery. A group of dejected, tousle-haired men in a variety of long underwear was lined up under the buffalo guns of Jacob and Samuel. They had clearly been driven from their bunks.

"This is what's left of the crew, Dan," hailed Jacob. "Reckon none of 'em are really dangerous. The worst have probably run for the border already, havin' too much sand to buckle under to Pringle and Terry an' knowin' the big money game was up. Maybe some of these jaspers are honest enough cowpokes experiencin' hard times an' the Major will want to keep 'em. It's all up to him. After all, it's still his outfit."

"Sure," grinned Herrick. "It's still his outfit."

"It sure as hell still is my outfit," emphasised a well known voice behind Herrick. He turned and saw Cal McDade walking towards him, a little unsteadily, but full of determination. Doc Grogan had improvised a bandage around his head.

The rancher snatched at Herrick's sleeve urgently. "Listen Dan. I want to say what I was tryin' to say when you were first here. I want you to come in with me in runnin' the spread — a partnership. That's what I had in mind when I wrote you. I wanted it as much as I wanted your help in settling the hash I got myself into. Sure, I knew I took a tiger by the tail when I imported gunnies an' I needed help in gettin' out from under. I needed you, Dan, even though I treated you pretty damned badly. I had no idea things were as bad as they were, though, an' that Terry an' Pringle were plottin' robbery."

Herrick shook his head. "I guess that's what you get for bringin' snakes on to your range — sheer poison. As for a partnership, Cal, it doesn't interest me. You need to rebuild, but you'll have to do it without me."

"Dammit, Dan, it's a handsome offer. You know this is a good outfit. At the end of my days, you'll get everythin' Elizabeth would have got," protested McDade. "She would've got it, anyway, even if she'd married you, no matter what war talk I made back then. That's why I didn't want these gunnies to kill you. I needed you bad."

"It's all too late, Cal. None of it will bring Elizabeth back. Get busy on findin' a new crew you can trust. An' you'll have questions to answer. We aim to telegraph the US Marshal in Tucson an' take Terry an' Cory to Benson so the Marshal's deputies can arrive by train an' collect 'em. There are charges of murder for the Holbrook killin' an', probably, Rogerson's death against Terry for sure. Cory's been involved in conspiracy at the very least as well as professional malfeasance."

"I was never involved in killin's," the rancher objected. "That was done by Terry an' Pringle for their own reasons, so there'd be no intelligent leadership among the sodbusters because they wanted to call the tune on these ranges."

Herrick leaned against the peeled pole fencing of a corral and massaged his stiff arm. "That's no more than you wanted yourself, Cal, though I'll allow you never tended toward murder in all the years I knew you. Maybe they'll get

220

the truth of the matter out of Terry in court."

"Hell, Dan, I might have trampled crops an' hauled down nester homes, but it was done after they'd been scared away. I never killed anyone, burned barns or pulled down the roof over a family's head an' I never ordered it. Who d'you think I am — another blasted Sheridan? I just used a few of the methods we used against Indians an' rustlers in the old Texas Long Trail days."

"Sure, but those days are gone, Cal. This country needs more than that. It needs the formation of a county, with properly elected officials. It needs a genuine peace commission an' a decent county sheriff with a real marshal in Centro instead of your old relic, Yawberry. An' it needs old Texas herders like you to reform in their old age an' somehow get respectable."

Cal McDade made a wry face and Herrick could not help smiling. For all his faults, the old rattler represented something resolute and strong. He had fought with all his might for what he believed in. He and his kind had done some good out here on the frontier, even if they couldn't understand that strong-arm methods had had their day.

Back in the days when the land was raw and the building was done from scratch, such men were the builders of what modern men called civilisation, rough as they were in their methods. But they were simple-minded and, too often, a younger generation of craftier men — or those of their own generation grown crafty and avaricious — came along with sophisticated means of stealing what they had built. It had almost happened to Cal McDade, but he'd withstood even a physical beating.

The rancher began to walk away towards the bunkhouse. "I'm about to pay most of them fellers in their underwear their time an' tell 'em to ride off my grass. Never failed to pay a hand what was agreed an' I ain't startin' now," he stated. "There's one or two worth keepin' on. After all, I have a cattle outfit to think of." His stride was steadier now. Though he had taken a fearsome pistol-whipping and was well along in years, he was still as tough as old hickory. He half turned his head and called back over his shoulder: "An' I'll lick whatever they throw at me in court!"

"I don't doubt that you will, you ornery old rannihan," murmured Herrick, hiding another grin with his hand. Then he shouted to the rancher's retreating back: "Thanks for fixin' Pringle for me, Cal. Only an old Texas trail man could have done it the way you did!"

★ ★ ★

The sun was well up when a buckboard, comandeered from the Walking C, left the ranch road and headed north over the dusty land.

Doc Grogan drove it while Hosea Candlin sat beside him, half-turned in the seat and watching the wholly subdued Terry and Cory, who were huddled on the wagon. Hosea nursed his big Sharps 40-65-330 in a way which was meaningful enough to the prisoners. At the back of the bunkhouse, the corpse of Larry Pringle who had called himself Lafe Pendexter, a relic of the longhair and quick trigger tradition who had now truly had his day, was stretched under a tarpaulin. Jacob Candlin rode immediately behind the wagon with both a buffalo gun and hard eyed determination which matched his brother's. Dan Herrick was astride his bronc beside the head of the wagon.

Samuel Candlin had remained back at the ranch to keep Cal McDade company. Most of the remaining gunnies were no-account saddle tramps who were ready enough to depart now that the easy money had dried up. Others, who were not dodging warrants, were willing to talk terms of honest, sore-rump cowboying if McDade had no objections.

The party of travellers aimed to make a stopover at the Candlin homestead for grub and to rest the horses, then press on to Benson. They would arrive around nightfall and telegraph the federal law authorities at once. Law officers should arrive by the next morning's train.

Doc Grogan that highly unlikely field commander who had learned his business with John Singleton Mosby, squinted into the sun and smiled with satisfaction.

"You know, boys," he declared, "we might be growing old and maybe we did fight on different sides all those years ago, but I reckon we all got the same kind of enjoyment out of that little ruckus of ours."

"Sure thing. It was just like the old days," chuckled Hosea.

"Amen," intoned Jacob from his saddle at the rear.

"Sure. Just like the old days," grinned Doc. "Still, better not wallow in memories of what used to be.

Otherwise, we'll wind up like old McDade, still with the rights and wrongs of the big war stuck in our craws. We have things to do. I, for one, have to give some thought to my patients."

They reached a fork in the trail. In one direction, the beaten track of earth ribboned off towards the Candlin claim while the smaller track angled off in the general direction of Dorcas' homestead.

Doc reined up to give the animals a rest and the party jingled to a halt.

The medico turned to Herrick, brushing back his moustache in his familiar, philosophical way.

"Speaking of other things to do, Dan. Seems to me these boys and I can manage this cargo of freight without you along." Behind his glasses, his eyes twinkled devilishly. "Isn't there something else you'd sooner be doing?"

Taken by surprise, Herrick murmured: "Well, if you're sure Doc — "

"Of course we're sure, aren't we

boys? Hell, it's still an easy chore for a couple of old Sheridan Scouts and an old Mosby raider."

Hesitantly, Herrick touched spurs to his bronc.

"Oh, and take care of that arm," declared Doc. "Keep massaging it. Seems like it'll trouble you for a while yet. It should be fine in time, though."

Herrick raised smoky dust along the narrow trail. He hoped Doc was right about the arm. He'd need it for hard work in the future, a future in which his gun would be put away for good. He thought about that future as he spurred the bronc onward. It beckoned him welcomingly. Maybe it would even bring his dream of a modest cow outfit in the Big Bend country of Texas to fruition.

At length, he rode down the slant of land at the front of the Holbrook homestead. From a distance, he glimpsed Dorcas at the window. Then the door opened and she came out, shielding her

227

eyes against the sun to watch him for a moment.

She started to run across the yard, out of it and up the rise. Herrick reined up, swung quickly down from the saddle and began to run down the slope to meet her. Dorcas continued running and spread her arms wide.

He thought suddenly of Elizabeth and felt a comforting assurance surge through him. He knew that, if anything of her ghost, her presence, her *chindi* existed, it was all about them, in the golden warmth of the sun, the clean blue vistas of the sky and the desert air and wind.

And he knew that she was laughing her joyous, silvery laugh — and fully understanding and approving the way he was now gathering smiling, panting Dorcas into his arms and kissing her hungrily.

***Other titles in the
Linford Western Library:***

TOP HAND
Wade Everett

The Broken T was big. But no ranch is big enough to let a man hide from himself.

GUN WOLVES OF LOBO BASIN
Lee Floren

The Feud was a blood debt. When Smoke Talbot found the outlaws who gunned down his folks he aimed to nail their hide to the barn door.

SHOTGUN SHARKEY
Marshall Grover

The westbound coach carrying the indomitable Larry and Stretch headed for a shooting showdown.

FIGHTING RAMROD
Charles N. Heckelmann

Most men would have cut their losses, but Frazer counted the bullets in his guns and said he'd soak the range in blood before he'd give up another inch of what was his.

LONE GUN
Eric Allen

Smoke Blackbird had been away too long. The Lequires had seized the Blackbird farm, forcing the Indians and settlers off, and no one seemed willing to fight! He had to fight alone.

THE THIRD RIDER
Barry Cord

Mel Rawlins wasn't going to let anything stand in his way. His father was murdered, his two brothers gone. Now Mel rode for vengeance.

ARIZONA DRIFTERS
W. C. Tuttle

When drifting Dutton and Lonnie Steelman decide to become partners they find that they have a common enemy in the formidable Thurston brothers.

TOMBSTONE
Matt Braun

Wells Fargo paid Luke Starbuck to outgun the silver-thieving stagecoach gang at Tombstone. Before long Luke can see the only thing bearing fruit in this eldorado will be the gallows tree.

HIGH BORDER RIDERS
Lee Floren

Buckshot McKee and Tortilla Joe cut the trail of a border tough who was running Mexican beef into Texas. They stopped the smuggler in his tracks.

BRETT RANDALL, GAMBLER
E. B. Mann

Larry Day had the choice of running away from the law or of assuming a dead man's place. No matter what he decided he was bound to end up dead.

THE GUNSHARP
William R. Cox

The Eggerleys weren't very smart. They trained their sights on Will Carney and Arizona's biggest blood bath began.

THE DEPUTY OF SAN RIANO
Lawrence A. Keating and
Al. P. Nelson

When a man fell dead from his horse, Ed Grant was spotted riding away from the scene. The deputy sheriff rode out after him and came up against everything from gunfire to dynamite.

FARGO: MASSACRE RIVER
John Benteen

The ambushers up ahead had now blocked the road. Fargo's convoy was a jumble, a perfect target for the insurgents' weapons!

SUNDANCE: DEATH IN THE LAVA
John Benteen

The Modoc's captured the wagon train and its cargo of gold. But now the halfbreed they called Sundance was going after it . . .

HARSH RECKONING
Phil Ketchum

Five years of keeping himself alive in a brutal prison had made Brand tough and careless about who he gunned down . . .

FARGO: PANAMA GOLD
John Benteen

With foreign money behind him, Buckner was going to destroy the Panama Canal before it could be completed. Fargo's job was to stop Buckner.

FARGO:
THE SHARPSHOOTERS
John Benteen

The Canfield clan, thirty strong were raising hell in Texas. Fargo was tough enough to hold his own against the whole clan.

PISTOL LAW
Paul Evan Lehman

Lance Jones came back to Mustang for just one thing — revenge! Revenge on the people who had him thrown in jail.

*